THIS PARADISE

We need voices to record and examine the strangeness and anxiety of living in the UK through such turbulence. *This Paradise* serves as a beacon of hope, a record of fear and an examination of these uncertain times.

—Alice Slater, *Mslexia*

The most original short stories I've read in a long time ... current, entertaining, and relevant. Highly recommended.

—Jimena Gorraez, *Litro*

The range of Cowling's style and subject matter is impressive ... *This Paradise* is a beautiful and highly original collection.

—Sam Mills, *The Spectator*

Ruby Cowling offers a call-to-arms, an urgent encouragement to breathe complexity back into a human experience made simple. We will be recorded, we will be flattened and reduced. But we can record too.

—Jon Doyle, *Review 31*

Most stories have their 'home' audience. But when fiction crosses that inner ring, and survives to tell its tale, well – that's art. And *This Paradise* achieves that handsomely.

—Tamim Sadikali, *Open Pen*

THIS PARADISE
BY RUBY COWLING

BOILER HOUSE PRESS

For my parents

EDITH ALEKSANDER, B.1929

When they tire of their fighting games, the children run into the sunroom, shouting, 'Dance, Nana, dance!'

I know if I refuse or wave them away, they will needle and nag and pull on my hand. So I make the long climb to my feet, wait for the shimmering veil to clear, and get into position.

Humming a wavering reed of a tune I weave around the living room, my limbs like twigs in a storm.

The children laugh and clap with the loveless delight of little gods.

It is a very, very long time since I was a child.

This morning, the youngest brought me a pair of tiny white wings her brother had pulled off a doll. She laid them in my palm and whispered, 'For you.'

'Thank you,' I said.

She ran off, her business done, already forgotten.

These children! Their love, their violence, so lightly despatched – you would think there was nothing that could leave a mark on them. I closed my hand around her gift and the wings seemed to tremble, buzzing softly in my palm.

I would love to have had wings. I could have soared, at ease, over the many decades of the middle of my life, instead of crawling and clawing like a low creature. I could have carried my daughter on my back, shown her landscapes from above, lit her small worried face with wonder. Or I could just have flown. Wings would have excused me from having to be present in the world.

1942. We, four other girls and I, had to dance for the Kommandant. We were fifteen, fourteen years old. Thirteen. We stood lamb-eyed before a line of guards, our tender bodies already going to bone. One by one we twirled for our lives while our audience clapped and laughed. The man's eyes sharpened, and he pointed, and I was chosen.

The girls I outdanced I did not see again.

So.

I remained a dancer. I made a living from the grace of my body; the curve of my neck won me applause, the tilt of my head won me suitors. I would stretch from shoulder to fingertip, filling the arm with light – and pause, and reach, and softly turn...

These lines and arcs of longing are what described my life. A young woman and then not so young, I had to move, move, move, forever pushed from the inside by that lump of undigested history. Something intimate to be expelled, to be sweated out, and yet it stayed dug in, stubborn and hot.

I could not marry, but from one of those suitors I bore a daughter. She came in a great bolt of joy, which, undeserving, I raged against. Every day as she grew, that fire of rage and joy made me fear for us both.

Somehow, the friends I made from stage and troupe and company were brave enough to stay my friends. Seeing me near a brink, each time they took my daughter in until the worst had passed.

'Oh my dear,' they told me, not knowing what it was that made me dark, thinking it was my exile, my slow struggle to master this language, 'time will heal.'

But I have been alive so long that time itself has become ancient – I have watched it happen – so I cannot rely on time to mother me. It has been too long, and I have lost hold of the end of the piece of yarn that will take me home.

On other days, waking to find myself still living, to find this world still just as furious, I begin to fear that time is, in fact, a circle.

And yet there is my daughter, my daughter. A child scarred by the fire I raised her in, and yet she had three children of her own, each one a layer of balm against the past. And now she brings me to *her* daughter's home, softens my chair with blankets, and they give me the blessing of the name of Nana.

I sat in the sunroom this afternoon and looked outside at the children playing, three of them pinning down the fourth, who afterwards picked up a stick and stabbed at the one who was slowest to run. The doll's wings lay in my lap. This morning's moment played in my head like music: her hand dropping the wings into mine, her chestnut eyes like a deer's. 'For you.'

Of course, she did not understand what she was doing. How could she? The tendrils of consequence uncoil beyond our understanding, ending at a place where joy and anger and desire stand silent and equal, free from the taint of blame.

Tonight, before the mirror, I twist the rope of my spine and press the white wings to my shoulder. They fasten to my flesh and grow, my heart at last unhooked from where it hung, and now I stand at the open window and know I am ready to go.

THE TWO-BODY PROBLEM

For J.

Esther

We are as close as we can
possibly be. In the time before
time starts, in fact, we are
one. In the crimson months
our twoness begins, but
we're enwrapped, encircled, a
singular pair.

Stella

We are as close as we can
possibly be. This is the
universe and we are staying
put. Distance does not exist.
Then we're pushed into the
shock of air and light and
otherhood.

How can we know, looking in a mirror, who we are looking at? We could ask the other but still not be sure. In private, I call her Stevie and she calls me Bertha. She seems more real than I am. In photos where we're asleep and bonny under knitted blankets, or chocolate-mouthed in high chairs, I think she's me and I'm her. It's her face I grew up gazing at, after all.

It would be easier if our names were less alike. The near-rhymes, the Est- and the Ste- that tangle on the tongue; they keep us tacked together like two joined hands. We try swapping names for a bit, but it freaks us out. We are two bodies, that's for sure – it's our doubleness that makes people look – but some force holds us, balances us, makes us one. Our own private force of *us*.

Thirteen summers swatting a Swingball round and round, waiting for something to change, then childhood falls behind us like a lifeboat cut adrift. She goes all Madchester, dying her hair, slouching round in baggy t-shirts and Docs. She stops bothering with 'pointless' lessons like RE – instead she strolls out of the gates, slinks into the park to do nameless things. She answers Mum and Dad back. Their faces make me curl up: I don't know how she dares. On the other hand, it keeps the heat off me.

Adolescence brings a choice. Hardworking, head down, obedient-to-survive? Or tell the world what you think of it, demand to know why you're trapped in this terrible place? It's not as if we discuss it, but I know she's sensing it too: change. She buys bras she's not ready for, playing with the straps so people see, and walking with this sort of sashay. She starts talking in a little baby voice which sets my teeth on edge, but at least in comparison I look like the cool one.

I stay clean, do more around the house, to stop our parents from going berserk. I know I'm trying to compensate, keep us balanced, keep us all right. But I can see her receding. It feels like being stretched and stretched and stretched.

Yeah, I drink, I smoke, so what? I want something that will taste of *me*. That desire has the sting of betrayal in it, but I can't say no. The taste of me is good. It's the taste everyone else takes for granted.

Something happens at a party
– it's boy stuff, bitchy trouble
from a so-called friend, and it
hurts. I try to find her, knowing
she'll stand up for me if no one
else will, but she shakes me
off, eager to leave me behind.

At this party in fifth form,
Esther won't stop bugging me.
I tell her and turn away, hard.
Later, I see her across the room
with a friend's arm round her
hunched shoulders, her soft
Bertha eyes red, her mouth all
twisted up.

At our leavers' do, with a little bit of careful manoeuvring, I finally get off with Barry. Fit, funny Barry, who looks at me like I'm a lovely surprise. I like that feeling of having someone to phone, to tell small things to; at last, someone who's on my side again. We make a tight couple, and though people say we're mad when we get engaged, I feel settled, balanced by him. I feel almost as if things are exactly as they should be.

Then she gets this boyfriend. He looks at her as if she's the only person in the world. She skips around saying she's going to marry him, and a sour liquid fills my chest. We're heading for the same uni (we both have offers; I'm not a complete waster) but oh, here's *Barry*, pulling everything good in his direction. We get our results, then she and Mr Centre-of-the-Universe choose Edinburgh. I choose Exeter. Four hundred and fifty miles is about right.

Edinburgh's fine. I do okay. Barry and I go home for the holidays, but never seem to coincide with Stella. Dad gets ill, then worryingly so, and I wonder why I hardly noticed him before. Or Mum, actually, who grows strong in the caring, then cracks, steps out of herself, goes beyond strong, becomes magnificent. All I can do is watch the pair of them, jealous.

Everyone thinks I'm running wild down here, but I've lost interest in all that. Mostly I stay in, staring at books on my reading list, remembering to be glad I don't have to share a room any more. My thoughts go dark. I get the feeling I've lost my grip on the thing that used to be at the centre, the thing that made me significant.

Mum and Dad are suffering, but together, pulling each other through the swamp of time. Each cares for the other in unspoken ways, easing the other's agonies with a look or a touch. Who do I have? I stand outside the closed door while they talk of private things.

I leave Mum and Dad's letters unopened for days, then skim them as quickly as I can. Over time their optimism turns to euphemism, through which the sadness leaks. *It's a great help when your sister visits*, they say. But if I went back I'd only bring everyone down.

Barry and I split up at the start of our finals, as the wedding begins to loom. In an awful midnight phone call full of silences, he makes me say it's not him, it's me. But it is him.

They tell me she's got a mobile now and send me her number, but I don't phone, and I stop phoning home: too many sorrys to say. That massive word is the weight that's keeping the lid on everything.

I realise being alone must seem normal to other people. Unpacking in my new flat, I flick through boxed photos: here's me on May Day, straddling the bike I covered in blue crepe paper, so proud of my work. I turn it over for the date and details Dad always wrote, only to find her initials, not mine. I feel a *fondness* – really, that flimsy – as if she's someone I knew just for a while, in another time. I'm thrown. I don't even know where she's living.

It becomes a struggle to breathe, as if I'm spinning into cold outer space. Somehow books don't hurt. I claw my way to a first, and Exeter offers me an MA place, fees paid, with a maintenance grant on top. So I do the obvious thing: I run off to Spain without telling anyone, get a job in a bar and a bed above it, and spend my days lying on the flat white roof, willing the warmth from our shared and distant star into my bones.

On our twenty-second birthday we are as far apart as we have ever been. I sleep in, treat myself to a manicure, have lunch with a few friends, do some job applications. It all helps to keep me busy. Then, at nearly midnight, I get a text from an unfamiliar number: Happy Berth-day! It's her.

On our twenty-second birthday we are as far apart as we have ever been. It's a raucous Saturday night at the Dos Soles and I forget the date. Then, between customers, I catch myself in the mirror behind the bottles. I meet the softening gaze of my reflection and raise an imaginary glass. It's her.

A few months drift by. In a post-chemo snooze Dad mumbles my name, but it comes out as hers. I get a gripe in my solar plexus, which I put down to a recent hospital-vending-machine egg sandwich. Then it doesn't go away. Things start to feel urgent, as if they're closing in.

Maybe because everything is moving all the time, there comes a point even if you run when you have to face the fact of your family: how to measure their influence, what to do with that measurement now that you know it and can't pretend you don't. Whether to reconcile or to let go.

She's not hard to find; she's still on her uni's message boards, calling herself Stevie. She writes straight away when I join. It's as if all it takes for us to start coming back is a small change of intention on each side, a reaching glance over our cold shoulders.

I wrestle with the reconcile-or-let-go thing until my therapist says, 'For God's sake, Stella, just stop resisting her.' Yes, I have a therapist now. Her advert in the expat paper said *Speaks Eng. & Sp., understands heartbreak in any language.* 'Make a gesture,' she says. 'You'll see.'

We're shy over email, then the phone, then suddenly we're together again, squeezing the death from each other at the airport. She stays in town and we see each other every day. Her eyes are rich and sad. My throat gets a rock when I realise: she's beautiful.

The whirl of arrangements and messages feels like quiet music getting louder, then suddenly we're together again. My Bertha: sort of wiser, but still so gentle, so natural. We help each other through the worst of everything, without many words. The closeness lasts a little while after Dad.

* *

So...

So...

This seems weird.

I know.

Dunno why.

Me neither.

I mean, it's you.

It's me.

And it's me.

And it's you.

It's us.

It's us.

I'm glad we did this.

Me too.

* *

We talk about work, share our silly dreams, but she looks out of the window when I tell her about the men I'm sort-of-seeing. Poor Stevie. I wonder if she'll find someone. I backpedal, tell her I'm not really looking, but the words feel cottony and weak. I'll always be looking.

We talk about me moving back, or whether she'd come to stay with me for a bit. We talk about going travelling together. Then we both go quiet. I remember what I've gone through alone, how hard-fought my solidity is, and I know what's happening. It's the other irresistible thing that's happening.

And then, soon enough, I
feel us drawing apart again.
My heart protests, fearing a
repeat. I hope this time it's not
that we are pushing off each
other, but more a healthy drift,
a letting go because we need
each other less. Or maybe now
we're not two bodies circling,
drawn and repelled by the
force of *us,* but two free souls
on a bigger, straighter course,
the serene unfurling of some
ungodded plan.

It can't be helped. Inside our
us, grown twins standing face-
to-face, we notice more that's
different than the same. This
thing can't be measured like
our height or feet or DNA,
but that doesn't mean it has
no mass, no pull of its own.
Even with the warmth of her
so close, even with a pull as
strong as the private force of
us, we can't stay still. We can't
stay in the same place.

We go back to our own lives,
no longer circling but each
pushing forward our long
line of days. Learning to work
with the damp clay of being
one, I make a decent fist of
happiness. The problem is to
recognise the path that's in
my name and only mine. To
turn my back and take it when
there's someone else to think
of, someone who's my closest
star when I'm her closest too.

Once we were each other's
only force, but later there are
other things that act on you.
Other orbits you can take, each
one spiked with its own pinch
of loneliness. It's a taste I've
got used to, perhaps it's the
taste everyone else takes for
granted. But out of nowhere
she can pull on me. Words
bring us back – *revolve, evolve,*
they're words for what we've
done, their hearts suggesting
love, re-love, re-love.

WE ARE PART OF THIS

I

We sit in our circle of twelve, working on our dolls, the dinky central fire doing its best against the April damp. Then Greta puts on her robe and leaves the tent to do her holy things and, as always, Phil follows. We stretch, look at each other, and scurry down to the illicit realm of chat.

We determine that a) today must be Tuesday; b) everyone has a battering headache (except Jeanette, who never touches caffeine); and c) no, it's not our imagination: the rain hasn't stopped since Sunday night. It was soothing at first, coming in waves, cycles, but its failure to stop – ever – has begun to feel personal. It's pittered, pattered, petered out only to peter back in. It's settled and softened to a radio fuzz, lulling us into stepping outside, soaking us through before we realise. At other times it's hardened suddenly, becoming a pelting, hammering harbinger on the put-upon canvas, and we've had to shout.

We've been on this camp since Saturday. We dream of hot showers, our own pillows, food you don't eat with a spoon.

Our breath is sour, and our clothes release wafts we're not happy about. We sit cross-legged ten hours a day and when we climb from the stream to the lodge on its hillock our knees throb horribly. And all thoughts lead back to this headache.

'Even if it stops raining today, I still don't know how we're going to manage on Friday,' says Doreen, who has one of those downturned faces. She's brought a little foldaway fishing seat we both scorn and covet. Primping the doll in her lap, she semi-sings, 'Mud, mud, drowning in mud.'

Friday's climactic festivities are to take place on the riverside paddock, which we can see if we stand on tiptoes at the firewood shelter behind the lodge, and peer downstream. It's already a steaming swamp. We don't know exactly what we'll be doing – it's been trailed only as a celebration of femininity: fecundity, friendship, general non-penile things – but we do know we will have to take the risk of expressing ourselves, perhaps through dance, or spontaneous poetry. We might have to take our clothes off. We're already referring to it as 'The Big One', and it looms like a bear.

Even the prep is daunting. We are weaving, carving, decorating. Forming, with our artless twenty-first-century hands, tiny symbolic objects made of wood, little stones, coloured thread, bits of leather: materials we've brought with us, saturated with private meaning. The objects are to help us expose what we hide, and since we're all doing it we tell ourselves that's fine.

This afternoon we have to make dolls, about eight inches tall, out of 'whatever feels right'. We're not sure anything feels right; nevertheless, our hands are busy. Apart from the odd tut of frustration, we've been silent. Now, with the leaders gone, it's a relief to check in with the others.

'My problem is I don't know what this is *for*, so I don't know what to make it look like,' says Jeanette, dangling her doll by the wool of its hair. She's a moon-pale woman with two thatchy plaits who keeps bursting into folk song.

'I think they're supposed to represent our younger selves,' one of us says.

'I think we're going to stick pins in them,' says another.

'Both,' say two of us at once.

Maggie thrusts at a scrap of scarlet velvet with an embroidery needle. 'Isn't this lovely, though? Being together? No men?'

We think of our husbands and partners and fathers and brothers and sons: those we've had; those we have; those we might have. Their bodies and beards, their clear, defined gestures. Their specific scents. We sigh, thinking we can't be heard over the rain.

We have each paid £500 for this week, and there have been mutterings about fortnights in Fuerteventura, but the grumbling is just a reflex. In fact, it's been an agonising kind of wonderful to spend a few days really away, with no mobile signal, without all the nagging screens. We're embarrassed at how 3D the world has turned out to be: full of scents and sensations, and stuff we didn't know we were missing. The un-switch-offable shufflings of insects and birds. The mist hanging paleolithic in the trees when we've stepped outside at dawn to pee. The cool stone of the carved goddess, weighty and voluptuous in our hands, signifying our turn to speak in a sharing circle.

Outside a circle, talking is tolerated but *chat* is forbidden. Now, after three days of relative discipline, we're weak with headache and have lapsed into three separate conversations: our offspring's career hopes; online air fares and their deceits; the use of arnica on pets.

'Daughters, PLEASE!'

Greta bursts through the lodge doorway. 'Ask of yourself: what you are saying RIGHT NOW, is it worthwhile of your breath? Does it HELP us? Are you even HERE? Tell me, do you want to LEAVE?'

Oh, yes please, we think.

Greta is our leader. Light bends towards her. She pierces the truth like she's spearing a fish. From the grit in her voice and the funny syntax we think she may be German by birth – but even thinking of her birth seems wrong: Greta was never, surely, some helpless, mewling baby. Every day she's gone off in her cedarwood-smelling robe to pray, coming back after a couple of hours somehow dry and un-dishevelled. While we fret and whine about our lives, our children, our jobs, mowing back and forth over our troubles, Greta stands over a problem and simply cuffs it away with a great paw.

And she is so, so, good to us.

'My sweet ones,' she says – gentle now, beaming now – 'if you like to leave, you may of course leave.'

Wha-? No! We wouldn't *dream*.

Greta's shouts have scorched the ground and left it clean. It's fair. We settle back to our dolls, so innocent with their blank faces. Then Phil shuffles through the doorway and talks for fifteen minutes about the value of silence.

Chubby, ruddy, stubby, Phil is Greta's right-hand woman. The side dish none of us ordered. In spite of her name, she proclaims her womanhood often, to the sky, wielding a twisted rod of white hazel, carved at its tip with what turned out to be an owl, though more than one of us had thought it was a penguin. On the first day we smirked, but something about her soon made us stop.

The silence lasts until Jeanette is moved to sing again. We wonder why Greta and Phil let her go on, when the rest of us are being such good girls, but they must know best.

II

Evening. We have spooned up bowls of grey barley broth and rinsed them in the stream, and are back in the sharing circle, shouldering blankets and dark robes, our hair left to fall free, hands hushed in our laps.

Nerinda is the oldest. She doesn't say much; we notice her because she pulls a glorious new outfit every day from an undersized hessian bag. She is seventh to speak. Our listening heads all tip at the same angle, lit only by the ever-moving fire and the stubs of loyal candle waxed onto its stone surround. Wet eyes glittering in soft ovals of face.

In her delicate accent, Nerinda tells a story about two mute swans in the Himalayas who, for thirty years, made circles on an enchanted lake. In their pair these two made solid the rippling water-world of *swan*. They hatched seventy-seven chicks and every chick was named, and, as the seasons turned, they fledged. Every year the parent swans were left to become two again, together with each other. The family opening and closing like a fan.

Then, one winter, the cold bit too hard and, as mist rose from the lake on a sunless day, the female swan nudged with her beak the motionless body of her mate. As spring came silently in, she swam on the lake alone, her reflection halved, lost into the water below.

We see, as we listen, the swan of the widow Nerinda. When she has finished and passed the goddess to Bernice, we sit for a time and watch the candlewax brim and spill.

Bernice is in her beautiful late teens and thin, her skin such a dark brown it's nearly black. The few times we've left the lodge and processed up through the village, she's the one the villagers are most agog at. We feel like lumps of putty next to her, but the way she thinks and moves and talks fills us with joy. We, who harbour horrors at who we were when we were young, listen to Bernice play the harp of her unbroken heart, and it makes us cry, hoping against hope that she'll stay this way forever.

Maggie takes the goddess. In the daytime Maggie asks us, 'Are you alright, lovey? Cup of tea?' She braves the rain to wash pots in the stream, tucks herself deep in the lodge with her arms round the latest weeper. Now she says she wants to travel the world, but her two younger sisters have some incurable condition that demands all her care and money. They will outlive her and her resources, unless she helps them die. Then she takes a very, very long pause.

It's just us and the rain.

We come to the end of the circle, stretch, sigh, desperate to pee. We push our heads through the lodge door flaps, pull faces of disgust at the collapsing skies. But what can we do? We shuffle into our boots and dash out, squat on the hillockside with our blankets tucked up, wait for our reluctant bladders to obey. Doreen's heels slip out from under her, and her cheeks slap into the mud. When she tries to get up she slips again, and her night-stark buttocks leave a groove in the muck as she skids down the slope and from the bottom she shouts, 'OH, BUGGER IT ALL,' and we laugh, laugh, laugh.

III

'Guys! Guys!'

It seems we've been asleep for only moments when we blink into the torchlight of pyjama-wrapped Bernice. The sheepskins beneath us are sodden, squeaking as we sit up in our bags and blankets. We scramble for torches, more of us waking, becoming indignant at the ruination. On one side we are sloshing ankle-deep in brown water.

'How can we be flooded, up here?' we say.

'The stream?'

'But the stream's miles down.'

'Makes no sense,' we mumble.

'God, the mess.'

'All my stuff... Everything's ruined,' says Maggie, hands aflutter.

'You can complain like little children,' smiles Greta, 'if your complaining will dry your cloths and put us back snuggling in our sleepy bags.' She is wringing out her things already, packing her bag. 'It is a not-lovely situation, but it's all we have. We must deal with, we must accept.'

We pipe down, focus on getting our things out of the puddles.

'Well, we're a bit stuck,' Phil mutters to Greta. 'We could try the village hall in the morning?'

'We go now. I have keys.'

'Ooh! How did you manage that?'

Greta lifts a casual shoulder. 'I have keys.'

We leave the dank tent, little ducklings following Greta through the streetlit village, the rain still mocking us, actually laughing as it falls.

IV

The village hall is a real building, with right angles. It has plumbing, radiators, ceiling tiles, and we feel as if we've stepped aboard a spaceship. There are health and safety posters, rumours of hot water in the kitchen. There's an actual toilet. We are so glad of these comforts, and yet... The Technoplast toilet seat is hard and unwelcome under us. So quick, this wilding. We are surprised when we glance in the rusted mirror under the fluoro tube. We peck our hands at our hair, rub a finger under our eyes, then give up.

We are marooned a second day. Yesterday's chard soup has improved overnight and someone finds some butter for our slice of bread. Jeanette starts up an endless round – something about a junior blacksmith and his sweetheart's grave – and we all end up joining in, even those of us who are not joiner-inners. Our headache, we notice, has gone.

Greta and Phil swoop in. The way they stand makes our singing stutter to a halt. We put down our work. Phil announces an emergency circle: five minutes. Nerves drive us to the loo and we exchange shrugs as we wait our turn. We settle back into a circle with a cloud over it. Greta palms the goddess.

'Someone – someone here – has been...'

She waits.

'"Tweeting".'

Her eyes sweep the circle. Minutes crackle by. The implications are hefty: not only does one of us have her mobile or other electronic device switched on and receiving, but she is narrating our private week to the wide world. The account is anonymous, Greta says, the worst sort of cowardice: the tweeter hiding while betraying her sisters, betraying everything that has depended on safety, confidentiality.

'So, I offer an opportunity to this "@shewolf65". Tell us – tell your trusting sisters – who you are, and explain why you have NO RESPECT for the sacred. NO RESPECT for the circle.'

In the silence we are all thinking of school assemblies, class detentions. We pretend we don't know you can get a mobile signal up here in the village – because we haven't thought to look, oh no, and absolutely definitely haven't checked for wifi.

Then we come to wonder how the betrayal was discovered. After all, to even *read* tweets, to know they're there, you have to – it must mean that either Greta or Phil –

Phil, it can't be denied, looks pale and uncharacteristically hunched. We straighten up, let indignation flare. Then we douse it with shame – for who are we to question Phil and Greta, and the rules of our retreat? So much depends on the rules. Our lives depend on these women, these mothers, being strong and wise.

The rain stops overnight, and we wake to an odd quiet.

Someone has placed a mug of camomile next to each of us. It's time for us to return, and we pack again, eager, speaking of the lodge as home. We have missed the dependable hardships of damp and draught.

Down the hill, we retake our abandoned camp. Water stains the flapping canvas skirt of the walls, as if the lodge has wandered, waded. The ground beneath our feet is springy and uncertain. But the flood has gone, the fire pit and the groundsheet are dry. We sweep, hammer pegs back into place, relight the candles. Rolling our bedding out again is like painting a wheel of colour radiating from the centre pit, re-illuminating a darkened scrap of the world. It's a good distraction from the way we're not looking each other in the eye.

V

On Friday morning, Nerinda has gone. Phil makes the announcement plainly, saying she was called home for an emergency. Something doesn't seem right in Phil's face. We keep noticing her and Greta exchanging long looks.

While they are on their holy walk, we whisper, stoking up the rumour that in fact our quiet, elegant widow friend has been sent away. Was Nerinda @shewolf65? We can't let it drop. Then there's a thud, and a hiss of exasperation from the other side of the canvas. We shush and fix alarmed eyes on each other. There's the half-sound, half-sight of someone moving off, a lightening of shadows we didn't know were there. Doreen mouths: *Phil.*

We carry on with our preparations, sombre now, thinking

of Nerinda, knowing it couldn't be her. We contemplate the dolls in our hands. What else do they need, our sweet little ones? Of course. Eyes. We blithely sew them on, until there they are, the eyes, staring back at us, the dolls dreadfully alive with their wordless understanding of everything we are. We hurry to zip them away.

Half an hour later Phil and Greta come back and tell us there's been a change to tonight's celebration plans. We're not going down to the paddock. The Big One will still focus on such concepts of the feminine as woman's strength and capacity for suffering, her deep-rooted relationship with the soil, the endless expansion of the fertile universe and so on, but the format will be different: they now feel ceremonial purposes would be better served by our facing these concepts alone, each on an individual journey to the underworld.

We exchange quick frowns and nervous quarter-smiles. The Big One is now much Bigger. We look down at our piti-ful collection of objects – the little stones we have daubed, the woollen nests of still-indeterminate form – which have taken on a sudden and terrible value. Somehow we know our survival may depend on them, and we note how badly they are lacking. We didn't anticipate being alone with our failures.

Under grey skies Greta and Phil lead us out into the woods, and we spend the day collecting a heap of rain-black-ened branches and twigs which we bend and snap and sort into piles divided by size. They show us how to stick the thickest deep and upright into the ground, weave the long thin canes around these pegs, and gradually build ourselves tiny cabins: one each. We pack the gaps in the walls with moss and spore-scented humus. They are strictly the size of one person sitting cross-legged, no more. We work in silence, and when we return none of us eats much of our chickpea stew.

VI

Dusk comes. We stand on spongy ground among beech and oak, spread out in a ring that keeps us six feet apart. We have been told not to speak, or turn around. Our backs feel open to whatever might come up behind us. The wind seems to raise anger in the leaves; it has a bite that gets through our clothes.

A long time passes.

It's getting harder to feel what the others are thinking as we shift and make little futile sounds in our throats to test against the falling night. The dark starts predictably enough but soon it goes too far, becoming improbable, falling through the ground. Is this what happens every night while we're safe in bed? The dark has a bitterness we can taste; *it's extra-dark, 100%-cocoa-solids dark*, we want to joke, because a joke is becoming urgent, but no words are possible, and we can no longer see enough of another face to seek reassurance. Our hands go to the handmade bags of objects slung across our chests.

We get thirsty. Our legs ache from standing.

Then steps approach, a type we don't know, and a tall shape hovers among the black trunks. It's holding something. The shape moves toward the circle. Some of us can see it coming and others can only hear it. We want to be sick.

The shape closes in, and seems to absorb one of us, one of us standing on that far side of the circle: we think it's Maggie. Maggie and the shape become part of the darkness. She goes with no sound, but someone else seems to whimper.

Another long portion of time passes, marked with the shuffling of leaves and night creatures, the odd human sniff. We think about drinking water, a lot.

Cloud continues to thin and finally a cold half-moon silvers the forest floor. In the lifted light we can now see four gaps in the circle.

We are not sure who is gone.

It was a mistake to come here. We've been tricked. Everything is wrong. The trees reel and lurch. The next thing we know the steps are coming behind us, and something grabs our shoulders and we are blindfolded and led stumbling away. Hands push us to our knees on the wet ground, pull our bags from our shoulders. Our faces are scratched as we crawl forward, then the wind is cut, the sound muffled, and the enveloping smell of damp forest debris tells us we have been pushed into the tiny cabins we built for ourselves. We tell ourselves we know the heavy, shuffling figures who are opening our bags and rifling. The intimate sounds of our dolls and objects being laid out on the ground before our crossed legs. The figures retreat, build up the door behind, sealing us in, and then we are alone.

How quickly and completely fear overcomes us is a surprise.

We rip off our blindfolds and there's still no light. The jagged twig-walls and ceiling are so close, we learn it's better not to reach out for them.

Though sitting, unmoving, we seem to contract and expand. Cold air needles through. Our lungs feel shrivelled, our breaths little puffs of bitter panic. We try to picture the others out there in their own cabins, but it's a flimsy image, faked, too obviously woven out of hope to be comforting.

In time we begin to sink. At first slowly, and then with a gathering weight, a gathering speed, we go down to a place we can't name, shrinking to the very seed of ourselves. The seed splits and something swims out; it's us, darting in a realm of shadow, flashes of threat on all sides: *hey you, you, you!*

Our heads get smaller while our bodies swell to fill the cabin and our own flesh starts to crush us. For a second it stops, when we realise it's not real, only to begin again when we ask what we mean by real. From the dark our dolls' eyes somehow snatch a flash of light, more alive than anything else around us, and how can we face that horror in here? But without them we are truly alone, so we have to swallow hard, cling to the hope that this is for the best and trust them. We grope for them, snatch them up and clutch them to us.

We are freezing. Someone is crying, then someone else.

Our lips are sore when we lick. If only there were some water. Time fails to pass: time upon time.

We think we can smell cigarettes, coffee. At one point we are sure we hear a Nokia ringtone. We think of Greta and Phil somewhere out there and think we hear them laughing. We will have plenty to say to them when this is over. Or have they gone and left us forever? Do we wish they had? We think of Greta and Phil and we think of our mothers, and whether we have any idea who they really are.

This is all wrong. But that's us. We are wrong all over. We are too selfish, too wild, too quiet, too pretty, too hairy, too different. We are too ugly, too boring, too chaotic, too lazy, too dark, too stupid, too clever, too rich, too common. Too manly, too girlish, too gangly, too weak, too gauche, too straight, too disorganised, too ambitious, too shrill, too needy. Too far away – irredeemably so – from what was expected of us.

To survive, we disembody, float up and look down and laugh at what's being done to us, but then there's vertigo and terror, and we scuttle back to our bodies and tough it out, and at last we are crying too, thinking only, *If I get through this; if I just get through this*.

VII

Then our cabin walls are torn apart, forgotten dimensions ripping open into a hole of freedom, and the dawn air rushes in so delicious and it's over. It's Greta and Phil free-ing us and we love them – of course, we love them: they are the most beautiful sight we have ever seen.

We help each other back to the lodge and gulp water. We are exhausted and alert, open as empty clams. Sweetness in the incensed air. Jeanette is paler than ever. Bernice can't stop shivering. Maggie hasn't spoken, or touched anyone. We don't know who we are any more, only that we are part of this.

It seems to be daytime, but the light is dim and the draughts coming under the skirt of the lodge are not benign. Someone has cleaned out the fire pit, scrunched up balls of paper and wigwammed clean kindling on top, like laid-out ingredients for a feast. We fixate on it, hungry.

The goddess takes many hours to go round, and no one uses the words *forest, dark, scared, desperate, wet, endless time, thirst*, or *cold*, because to do so would be to make small the big things that have happened. It would mean we didn't really survive anything. It would mean we really had been tricked.

One of us speaks, passes the goddess. Our eyes on the dormant pit in the middle.

The next speaks, passes the goddess.

Doreen speaks next. Shrugging deeper into blankets and shawls, we gaze to the middle with our listening faces. Then, as she is speaking of her children, yet not of her children, and of her death, yet not of her death, a flame woofs into life under the pointed kindling. We blink, imagining it. But no, it's fire, real fire: crawling sparks are blackening the paper, and it builds to a tigery triangle, and then it's real heat we feel on our doubt-filled chests.

Mutters crescendo. Who did this? Who lit this? We look at Phil, at Greta, at each other, for signs of trickery, but if there are signs they are not visible to the naked eye.

Our thought-gears click back in and start to turn, and we remember the village hall, the stark accusations of a breach of trust. No one has admitted to being @shewolf65. It wasn't Nerinda: come on, we know this now. But our hearts won't go any further down the path of accusation, even though our minds do; even though we know Greta has covered up her deputy's indiscretion and done so at the cost of all our purity. We steal glances at our two mothers, trying to see beneath what they show, hoping not to.

Why would they want to fool us? Everyone was gazing into the middle, watching all the time, and no one's been near the fire. It just happened, like magic. But there's no such thing as magic.

On the other hand.

We have seen so much that can't have been real. Maggie, among others, has seen age come over her: her skin growing too large, her hair becoming spiderweb, her knuckles Halloween frights. Doreen, among others, has seen a child, an actual person, sliding out of her own body. Jeanette, among others, has seen her father struggle for his last breath. All we agreed to in our contract with life was for time to slip quietly forward, and instead we've collected a heap of stuff too big to deal with, too unacceptable to accept, the weight of it often too much.

Now we're expected to believe in a fire that has come from nothing. Well, a week ago we had never met, and now we love each other.

The fire grows and the small pile collapses onto itself. The fire is real.

Maybe the joke is on us, but we'll take it, we'll add it to the heap, like our mothers' fallibility, like an ugly doll made from scraps that saved our lives in the dark.

We realise this miracle must be fed. Each of us leaps to a task, scrambling out to the shelter for dry wood, or lying on our fronts blowing pokers of air. Candles are replaced. Water is fetched; tea is made. Drops start to fall again, then quicken, and with the rain back it's as if we're really home.

It's all a paradox, this week of metaphors that were in fact literal things: the impossible fire; the strangers who became our mothers. We put ourselves in their hands, and they probably weren't who they claimed. We trusted and were betrayed and we kept trusting anyway, and it turned out okay. It was unacceptable, and we accepted it, because our lives are already stacked with the literally unacceptable. We just stagger on, beneath. As we go on, we have no choice but to let ourselves fall: to fall for each other and for the fine, fine mess of it all.

MATING WEEK

Adult Luna moths have a week of life: to mate, lay eggs, and die. Last weekend, fourteen of them struggled at last from their cocoons, taking a pause for the blood to pump into their pale green wings, then took to the air. For the last two nights, they've flitted around the storm lamps that light Sarah's moth house, creating indoor lightning that crackles the cool air as she works. But tonight, as she opens the back door and flicks on the switch, she sees that all but one have disappeared.

She raises them from eggs imported from the States, and for months she anticipates these few nights of frantic, mysterious company. When they die, she usually finds their bodies on the white gravel floor of the moth house, down amongst the huddled pots of young birch and alder. She picks them up carefully by the tip of a foot, the bodies paper-crisp and lighter than air, then carries them gently out to the garden to return them to the soil. Now, though, kneeling to rake her fingernails through the gravel and into the underdirt, she finds nothing.

She built the moth house herself, from panels of black mesh stapled into balsa uprights. A small extension, bracketed by her neighbours' clean glass conservatories, it juts into the tiny walled garden at the back of her terraced cottage. Beyond the garden is a patch of urban wood: for a while, an owl used to call from some high branch back there as Sarah worked. Then there were two, calling to each other; and then, after a few days, she didn't hear them again.

A nursery area just inside the back door is where she hatches the eggs, feeds the growing larvae and harbours the silent cocoons. She works, wearing several jumpers and fingerless gloves, at a wallpapering table against the brick back wall of the house, a bar heater at her feet when the nights are cold enough. Her movements are so small as she works – sometimes with acrylics, sometimes oil, sometimes pencil – that the moths come to rest for a moment on her hair. They're beautiful, of course, in their short and glorious mating days, but her artistic interest is in the fleshy little concertinas that are their caterpillars, and their long, secretive days of pupation. Even so, discovering the disappearance of the adult moths tonight feels like both a mystery and a quiet disaster – a maddening intrusion, even though it's an absence. Something has bothered her all day; she wonders whether that itchy feeling was foresight.

Working at night in the moth house, she's free from the daytime jangle of the phone: her agent, her toddler-tied friends, the over-bright world inviting her to come and account for herself. Today, though, no one phoned, and the four o'clock air grated with a silence so abrasive she was driven up to her bedside bookcase, seeking the balm of poetry. *In my dreams I am always saying goodbye and riding away.* When Stevie Smith failed to calm her, she took out her mother's few bits of jewellery – a pair of drop earrings shaped like short stems of ivy; an Edwardian ring with a filigree band, which her mother wore as her wedding ring though it was outmoded even then – and rubbed at them hard with the silver polish.

She leans into her drawing, uneasy now that it's just herself and the one remaining moth, who silently panics the air around the middle lamp. She is sketching a late larva, fat and spiny and masked with brown. She hopes that there may be eggs already, that at least there's been time for mating before the moths died. No bodies, though: they can't have died. But what, then? Her thoughts flit in small, stuck circles as she makes and re-makes her tiny pencil marks on the creamy paper.

Unsold works are propped six-deep against the studio wall. Her agent has started to get restless, phoning almost weekly.

'People want to look at nice things, I'm afraid,' he says. 'The looks on their faces when they see your stuff...'

'I know,' she says. Her squirming, bristling larvae and ghostly crosshatched cocoons are not what people want on their walls. 'I just – this is what I have to do at the moment.' She's reminding herself as well as him; what money there was left from her mother's house is long gone, and the need for a proper income will soon drown out the artistic imperative.

'Darling, of course. But while you're in this little phase, how about some pretty ones of the butterflies themselves?'

She's told him *moths, not butterflies*, ten times already. She bites back the explanation and rings off.

Even she doesn't know why she's so involved with this sub-ject – the barrier of the logical *why,* springing up unbidden, stops her even finishing a lot of these pieces – and she won't know until she gets to the end, whenever that might be.

The larva's almost-invisible hairs and toes make her squint and her head aches by the time daylight comes. The phone rings in the kitchen. She's glad of the interruption, stretching her arms and massaging the back of her neck as she goes in.

The hello comes out properly on her second try.

'It's me,' says the caller. 'Oh, just a sec –'

Sarah can hear two small combative voices deep in the phone's aural space, their words tumbling over each other and over Melinda's entreaties: 'Nicely, Grace, let Jack – shh, now that's not nice, give it to Mummy. Give. Grace. Jack, stop it.' Everything in here is just as Sarah left it. She knows exactly how much milk there is in the fridge, and the bat-tery in the wall clock still needs changing. The clock on the microwave says 08.07.

'Hi,' comes a breathless voice in Sarah's ear. 'What were you saying?'

'You rang me.'

'Oh yes. Not too early, I hope? They were up at five today. Just wondering how you were, you know, and to remind you about tonight. *Jack!*'

'Tonight.' She eyes the calendar, which still displays the lilac-and-lemon posies of April. Flipping it over quickly, she realises today must be Thursday 5th, as there's a scribbled —

'Hold on a sec.' Melinda goes distant again as the two small voices rise.

— a scribbled note, *Mel & Steve's 7pm.* They want her to

meet some work friend of Steve's, she remembers, and she suddenly feels tired.

Melinda comes back. 'Sorry – I've got to go. See you about seven.' She puts down the phone before Sarah can say anything.

She notices the kitchen bin needs emptying, counts nine mugs next to the sink. She must do something about the skirting board over there. Pulling on rubber gloves and swilling the fluffs of old tea down the sink, she hums, but the sound seems out of place and her throat is dry.

A life alone. Her mother used to use the phrase like a curse, but there's beauty in its assonance, its internal rhythm. It makes Sarah think of an owl's cry. She sees her friends *all the time*, she always assured her mother, though it's true that as they've staggered into their thirties and beyond it's become more difficult to fit socialising around the need to prepare lunchboxes and uniforms and get some sleep. Sarah is always pushing back a chair, saying goodnight, she must love them and leave them, get home to the studio and get something done. This is why she likes Stevie Smith. *I am glad, I am glad, that my friends don't know what I think.*

Night Waves is on the radio on the drive home. Steve's friend turned out to be a type her mother would have approved of; in spite of that, Sarah likes him. Scottish, graceful mover, steady eyes.

'Tell Ray about your paintings,' Melinda had prompted as she carried a sleepy-eyed child up the stairs. Steve was clattering in the kitchen.

'Actually, they're not paintings,' was the first thing she'd said to Ray, correcting him for a mistake that wasn't even his. They talked for a while about her moths. The warmth of his interest meant she was willing to go into more detail than she usually would – and somehow, without saying a word, he made her feel an unexpected delight in it all. It was simply his amused expression, as she told him how the larvae start off sociable and then become more and more solitary as they grow – she could see the way he was person-ifying them into little characters in his mind, making a tiny soap opera of their inching lives – and the funny side of her work transmitted itself from his mind to hers, and there it was, a whole new perspective to lighten her long nights.

She felt a similar little leap – that same freshness under her skin – when he said, as they sat down to eat, 'I'm just an idiot, I know, but there's something I've never understood about art. I mean, making something that just looks like something. Why?'

Mel and Steve raised eyebrows at each other, fearing controversy, but Sarah said, 'No, he's fair enough. If it just mirrors another thing, to me, it's pointless,' and she and Ray shared a look that she couldn't hold for longer than a second.

He had hardly talked about himself in the usual curric-ulum vitae way, and neither had he bothered with any duty questions about where she came from, or what she liked doing in her 'spare time', but it seemed already as if they were co-conspirators, kids who'd seek each other out in the playground. Mates.

When he did talk about his own work, in computers, she was surprised how interested she was. Unlike Steve, he was happy at the company; Steve said – not for the first time – that his kids were his life, that work was just a means of feeding and clothing them, and Mel had nodded and squeezed his hand. Ray was working on something about *persistence*, which he said was a quality your data gains when you tell the machine to save, that is, make a record, until which point it doesn't exist. Although she didn't fully understand how his project was finessing this idea, the idea itself pricked her.

But Steve had leant in and quipped, 'You'll need persistence with her,' and then one of the children was heard padding around upstairs and since they'd finished dinner Mel took Sarah up to say a final goodnight – for they are fond of each other, Mel's children and Sarah – and they didn't go back to the topic.

As she was pulling on her coat after coffee Ray asked for her number, and she gave it to him. But now, slowing to turn off the main road, she's not sure. It's a lot of trouble. You say you'll go for a drink and then after a few months you're sitting straight-spined on separate halves of the sofa blurting horrible gobs of truth at one another and someone starts crying, and it's back to square one.

Once she's pulled into her drive and roughly lined up with the letterbox on the front door, she turns off the engine. There's silence and darkness and she takes a moment – as she likes to do – to savour the fact that no one knows exactly where she is right now; it's as if she *isn't* actually here, and for a few heady seconds she is unchained from the world.

She allows the car to tick to stillness. To give up these moments would be costly. But half of her turns back and says wait, never mind *chained*, what about *connected*? What if, just by meeting someone, you've left a record of yourself on their mind, so now you exist whether you like it or not, and there's nothing you can do about it, and – her mind gropes haltingly in the dark – *what if that's okay?* A different headiness comes then, from a chink that's suddenly open and letting in a feeling like a breeze on her skin.

In a dream that night, she's back on her knees in the moth house. She pulls aside the drainage stones under the planters, finds nothing. She shoves through the lower leaves of the young birches, tipping the planters to climb further in. Then she sees something stuck to the underside of a large leaf, hanging there as incongruous as a third ear. It's a cocoon – a moth's – but it shouldn't be out here; she takes care of all those stages in her array of plastic pots and old cordial bottles in the nursery. It's also larger than normal: fatter than her forefinger and nearly as long. She sees another one clinging to a stem, and now look – there are a handful, a dozen. Another pupation is taking place; inside these cocoons the moths are remaking themselves a second time. There's a split in the first cocoon already and she can't resist; gently holding the leaf, she pulls a nail down the split and opens it up. Instead of the moist folds of a new moth, what's inside is dry and white. A scroll of paper. With her nail, she hooks it whole out of its brown shell and it drops to the ground. Her hands are shaking but she picks it up and unrolls it. On the paper are faint markings, not much more than whispers, but they form a familiar image. The most familiar image, in fact: the shapes and outlines of her own face.

When Ray hasn't phoned by Monday, Sarah gets restless –
and then annoyed at that restlessness, like a bite on top of
a bite. If she could admit it, she'd say it was the old clamour
for a mate, unwelcome and unhelpful but maddeningly
compelling. Since the dream, she's been flowing, finishing
her drawings, but the quiet nights are making her shiver.

Things were fine, before. For the last four years – four
richly productive, friendship-deepening, freely-breathing
years – she knew where she was, what the limits of her world
were, and this meant things stayed fine. So even though
she's known other restless days, in which she allowed her
mind to flit up against the boundaries, feeling out toward
what else there might be, they've only ever reaffirmed the
rightness of staying where she is, on her own. Until now,
of course, because of the chink that's been opened. Which
is actually nothing to do with Ray, the man himself – she
knows that much. It's just the possibility of change. It's the
inevitability of the next phase, when part of you has been
invisibly transforming all the time.

Starting her day, in the warm May glaze of 5pm, she
takes more care than usual clipping new sprigs of leaves
from the growing alders and misting the larvae's tubs with
water. She's bothered by the frass on the sheet under the
tubs, and she gathers it up and presses it into the washing
machine, adding the kitchen tea towels. She hesitates, then
goes upstairs and strips her bed. Turning to come backward
down the stairs, she bends and sweeps away the rolls of dust
step-by-step with a pillowcase.

Dustpan and brush come out, and a damp cloth and
a pine spray and the hoover. By nine, she's attacking the
spiderwebbed corners of the moth house. She pushes a

stepladder through the greenery and climbs to where roof mesh meets wall mesh at the wooden frame. The heat up here is surprising. It muffles things. Then she feels a slice of cool air moving her hair against her neck, like something whispering to her. She touches the skin where it's brushing, and follows the invisible rope of air to the shadowy panel of mesh in front of her. There's a hole. This is where they've been going. Her moths haven't been dying; rather, they've been flying away from her to spend their few days in freedom. Drawn out, when her storm lamps were dark, by the streetlight at the end of the row, or by the strong spring moons, they've been sensing the slim corridor of air by temperature or sound or some mysterious moth-knowledge – it was probably as obvious as a motorway to them – and taking this little doorway into the rest of the world. As they have every right, she supposes as she retreats down the stepladder, to choose to do.

With the end of June come short working nights and a reckless abundance of daylight. Sarah knows she's losing nothing when – after some cautious texts followed by phone calls almost adolescent in length – she agrees to an evening picnic with Ray, because she doesn't need so much night any more. The moth works she's finishing will be her last, and although she never perfected the pencil drawing of the caterpillar, it was recognisable at least; she got it down. There is something of hers to see now. Something that will stay as a mark of this time, whatever flickering risk she is about to take.

She has talked her agent into taking all her moth works for a joint exhibition later in the summer. Maybe she'll ask

Ray to come to the opening. What she will show there ought to be enough: her long-flown creatures in their former state, persisting, as if she still held them cupped precious in her hands.

THE GROUND IS
CONSIDERABLY DISTORTED

I was weeping after midnight, at the airport all alone. Suitcases turning and turning and never mine. But also: my mother, the abandonment, my annoying fever and cough, and my hard work, and the travel tiredness, and I am empty.

KNTN have sent me to UK to cover the politician's wife disaster insult story which is big now. My first time here and I have promised myself: write English, speak English, think English. But it is *strange*. Kurume was heavy with cherry blossom when I left, it seems years ago, but in London when we landed and walked for twenty minutes along halls there was not one tree to be seen outside. The passport lines were long and I waited, trying to send email from my phone, but it said Event Failed. I tried Twitter. Event Failed. Then when I got to Baggage Claim at last, my suitcase event failed there too, and I sat on the floor and wept. But then I thought of the Tōkai, and all the suffering on TV since, and also many English people were looking at me crying, so I stopped.

An Indian man gave me printout to bring back tomorrow for my suitcase, and I took tiny short train and then another train to London Paddington and the hotel my boss reserved, a Hilton. On the train was a TV weather and micronews repeat I mostly understood – certainly I knew pictures of Kakegawa and other ruined places of blood-and-dust-covered people – then a report outside the disaster-insult politician house, then they moved to Zurich nuclear summit and talked too fast for my ears.

Thanks, Huw. Nothing's been seen of the minister or his wife today, as you can see behind me the curtains are *closed* and they are not coming out or coming in or out of the house, as I say, no one has seen of… seen either of these two let's say contro*versial* become rather contro*versial* figures, or their advisors today, and the last word we have is still Monday's comments by their spokesman which as you'll remember were not too, not too well-received by the authorities concerned. In fact Huw some reports, there were some who felt the statement only in*flamed* the situation, only worsened the –

Yukako Inoue @yukai1988 3 Apr
@h_inoue7 Hi from London! I am at Paddington-Bear station :-) Please call home, otōto-chan…

At the Hilton my room is a box of quiet. I lie down and cough, then sit up when a white envelope slides under the door. It is a nice message from a Nick, from the camera pool at KNTN London office, offering welcome and giving a phone number, but it is so late. In five hours they start serving breakfast, and I look forward. I have a cool shower and my annoying fever eases a little, and I do some small work, though I pay £15.99 for Wifi, though my boss will pay.

He gave me instructions for this trip in an email, writing in the last bullet, *Relax and enjoy*. I am not good at this, it's true. Work is easier than fun. But he makes me wonder recently, touching my shoulder and leaning over to use my mouse. When I say his name at home my mother sniffs the air. Better for me to come here for a while. I wish she understood, but we are fighting again because of this trip.

I send some tweets in best reporter English. I even tweet my brother in English because when I try he smiles. Hajime's English is super perfect. It is dark now but not raining and if tomorrow is sunny, then hope springs, as English say, and with open curtains I lie on the bed and watch the big city morning come close.

When the breakfast opens I am so hungry even though I ate every peanut from the minibar. I take the elevator down to G and sit where I can watch TV news. So far London noise is just like Japanese city: screens talking all around. Breakfast is small rolls and an egg and nice jam and tea, and I cough only little. My closing eyes tell me the time to sleep is now. Annoying. But I am sitting by the window and the sun is warm. Later I will go to KNTN office at Piccadilly, then nice Nick and I will go to the house of Graham Pike/Susan Pike. But first I must adopt my suitcase, so I send Nick short sorry text, hoping this is okay in England, and get ready to leave for the airport again, though not hurrying because they said to come after nine.

When I look for email there is nothing, and I tell myself no looking for email for fifteen minutes, but I look. Empty. It is silence she uses.

My mother is waiting for me to get a husband so I can make a home and she can come and sit in a chair in corner until death. Hajime went 2,000km to Sapporo to do research at the Hokkaido University, which was a big surprise when he said he would not return, as he is my two years younger brother and I thought my turn would come first. But no, I am still in Kurume, where there are no boys to look at, and if I go on a work trip mother goes to bed for two days and says, 'Chest paining, stay and look after.' This time she asked, did I want her to die alone without me when the next earthquake comes, this time on Kyushu Island and it is our Genkai plant that cracks and leaks to the sea and sky, and in the wrong voice I said, Kyushu won't get an earthquake but of course mama, I want to die here with you. There was silence for a whole day, and I said sorry but it was like water on a hot stone. I am the unfilial daughter like my father called me once.

Back then my mother put arms around me, whispered to my hair that I shouldn't listen. Back then she would rub my shoulders when I coughed, bring me cool things for a fever. Her scent of clean like a stream running through gardens. This is everything I miss.

I owe so much to her and I feel warm when I do what she wants. But yet, there is my life to come as well.

– distance himself from what is becoming a very difficult, a *thorny* problem in his, in his side… especially with the NR Summit, the energy talks at such a critical stage as they were when the original, the comments were made, just hours after the earthquake struck on-on… in the early hours of Friday and the damage to the reactors at Hamaoka was becoming apparent.

But at this point, with as you can see *no* immediate developments, we'll just have to wait and see. Huw now it's back to you in the studio.

Graham

2020-04-03 23.24
OK. We will talk tomorrow.

2020-04-04 09.08
Are you coming out
at some point?

09.10
Good morning to you too.

09.11
Think I'll just stay
here today

09.11
Grow up, Susan.

09.13
Have you any notion
of how much trouble
you've got us into?

Graham

09.14
Yes that's why I'm staying
here. Also getting a cold

09.20
Thanks a lot for
your support

09.22
You know the pressure
I'm under w/ Zurich.

09.23
I'm just asking you to
do the right thing.

09.25
The right thing... Hmm,
long time since you saw
things so perfectly b&w

Graham

09.26
Please don't start.

09.27
I just think you can't
really ask me to look at
my conscience without
looking at yours re NR

09.32
And by the way,
we are texting

09.33
???

09.33
We are texting each
other in the same house again

09.34
Remember what Sylvia said

'Well, come out then,' Graham says, tapping with an exasperated knuckle. She shoves back the duvet and unbolts the bedroom door, tying her dressing gown as he comes in. The TV shows Hamamatsu and Kakegawa, collapsed, the series of unholy shots familiar as an advert.

'Can you turn that off?' her husband says.

'What's up? Too much Realism? Thought you were pro?' But she hasn't really got the energy, ha ha, to restart this argument, and the sarcasm sets off her cough.

'The thing is, Susan,' he says, as she jabs the remote, 'it's not like it used to be. You say something these days and if there's any *hint* of it being a bit off it goes whatsit, like an epidemic, it's everywhere in two minutes.'

Last week Susan Pike walked into a nightmare. Or a minefield, or a shitstorm: something that sounded like a metaphor to everyone else but which was in fact exquisitely real for the woman herself. But the whole thing was misunderstood. A molehill. In a teacup. Praj advised it'd blow over after his 'throwaway-remark out-of-context' statement, but so much for that. Now it's down to one thing: a direct and full apology. And she *is* sorry. But not in the way they think she should be.

'Look,' says her husband, 'you probably didn't mean –'

'Anyone who knows me *knows* I didn't,' she says. 'I mean, Jesus Christ.'

He winces. 'You see, that's what I mean.'

'What?'

'That kind of thing. *Language*, Susan. Thinking about it, using it. You can intellectualise all you like in private, swear, whatever, but out there, words mean something else.'

Her throat gets hot and hard, like in their sessions

when he'd be on his high horse, lecturing both her and Sylvia. Sylvia would only say, 'I'm noticing some reaction to what Graham had to say, Susan?' And when Susan once asked her if she agreed he was condescending to them both, perhaps because they were women, she got, 'What is it you feel about being a woman in this relationship, Susan?'

'I *do* think about language,' she says. 'I'm sorry people don't always take it the right way.'

'It's just a question of *thinking* about other people. Before you speak.'

'OK.' *Thinking about other people!* She has brought up three children! She heads into the bathroom.

'OK what?'

'OK.'

'That's all you have to say?'

'That's all I have to say,' she calls, with a mouthful of foamy toothbrush, and it sounds chirpy instead of authoritative, and she closes her eyes, defeated, and wonders how it is she's so often double-crossed by the sound of her own voice.

When she opens her eyes Graham is standing in the doorway, not finished with this. That's his way. She remembers him at twenty-two, hot-eyed with radical thought, in love with her enough to hide her car keys so she couldn't go home. When he forged her signature to commit her to the party, he said, 'It's just so we can be together *all* the time. It's all that matters.' It seemed sweeping, romantic.

'Praj is right, Susan. You have to do a straightforward apology.'

Still brushing, she shakes her head. 'Nh-hn.'

He rests a gentle hand on her rounded back.

'Darling. I haven't brought this up before,' he sighs, 'but this is hurting the kids.'

'I-n-o-u-e,' I tell the woman slowly, and point to the printout. 'Yukako Inoue.' I almost say *from KNTN* like my camera sign-off. She goes through a door and comes back pushing my suitcase and a feeling like love comes to my chest to see it.

She checks the suitcase label. 'You from Japan, then?' she says.

I nod.

She presses her lips together, sad. 'Awful, it's awful. Is your family...?'

I smile and tell her it's okay, I come from Kurume. Her face does not change, so then I say Kurume's a long long way from the earthquake, different island altogether. 'It's fine,' I say. 'Thank you, bye-bye.' Back to you in the studio.

But my insides are gripping, like when I tell my mother something not fully true. It is not fine. I'm trying to make mine a life of doing right, and now I hear my mouth say *fine*, as if it's fine for children trapped in rubble to die of thirst, for a nuclear plant to break up somewhere on another island. As long as my life is okay. That right there, the world's whole big problem that made me a reporter in the first place, is in me too.

I email to my mother, tell her I arrived safe. To make her see my trip is not nothing, I say how the Pike story affects Zurich and Zurich affects the whole world, especially Japan where we see safe nuclear is maybe not so safe. I tell her, the future means everyone must think of each other and of next generations. I write in Japanese of course but it is still hard to make it so she does not read it wrong.

Yukako Inoue @kntn_yukako
2 mins

Japanese #NRS delegates claim "sabotage" of laptops, hard drives, overnight: 8 of today's speakers unable to appear. More as it breaks.

Yukako Inoue @yukai1988
1 hr

So happy to have my clothes and things, thank you #Heathrow! @h_inoue7 did you call home yet? Please update!

Yukako Inoue @kntn_yukako
1 hr

BREAKING: UK PM to make public statement from #Zurich on Susan Pike #Tōkai comments. 12noon CET.

Yukako Inoue @kntn_yukako
3 hrs

Day 3 #NRS #Zurich & speakers opposing NR due to take stage.

Good afternoon. OK. Can we go?

Almost one week ago, the British Foreign Secretary and his wife attended a private charity event at the Palace of Westminster. At that event, Mrs Pike made some comments relating to the terrible and tragic events in Japan, which caused widespread offence both that evening and in the following days. Though the dinner was at Westminster and Graham Pike was arguably appearing as a representative of this Government, I would like to make it clear that Mrs Pike's comments in no way reflect the position nor the sentiments of my party or my Government, and furthermore they are naturally abhorrent to the large majority of the British public, as shown by the coverage in the British press this week.

It is with regret that I note the matter may be affecting relationships here at the Nuclear Realism Summit, especially with my esteemed colleagues representing Japan, as this is a unique opportunity for global leaders to focus on the real issues, and the real science, behind our nuclear future, and a unique

'Hamaoka? I think it's hilarious,' Susan said, and the table went quiet. 'Well, I mean, switch the reactors off for a year, build a billion-dollar wall, and switch them back on, everything hunky-dory. What did they think was going to happen when the Tōkai came? That wall was dust in about ten seconds.'

It was one of those dinners in one of those rooms, somewhere in the warren of the upper house: oak-panelled walls, oak-smoked salmon, oaked Chardonnay. Early on, Susan realised with alarm that she couldn't begin to remember the names or offices of anyone on her table. Names and offices used to be her superpower. By coffee, unable to draw out the other guests with pertinent questions, she was hearing a lot of her own voice.

Three places around the eight-person table, a Chair of something, bearded and soft-spoken, picked up his glass. 'I'm sure it was much worse than anyone anticipated.'

'It was a Tōkai earthquake, for goodness' sake,' said an Assistant Director, on her right. 'It was always going to be worse than anyone anticipated.'

'I'd hardly say any of it was *hilarious*,' muttered the council leader next to him, stirring and stirring her coffee.

'Oh God, obviously, the whole thing's horrendous,' said Susan. 'Four months earlier and they'd still have been shut down. I mean, such a big earthquake's bad enough – what are they saying, have they got to a hundred thousand now? – but for the power station to go as well...' Shaking her head, she reached for her dessert wine, but the glass was empty and she remembered her hand had already made the same fruitless reach a minute before.

Opposite Susan was a quiet, flushed woman with black-and-white-rimmed glasses, checking her phone under the table. These dinners could be an awful trial if you were an introvert. Susan wanted to bring her into the conversation, but how to start? The little place cards should face out, to the rest of the table, she thought, like at a summit. After all, you already know your own name.

Graham had been seated at the top table with the host, Lord Darby, a couple of ambassadors and a famous actor. Leaning in to listen to the formidable Lady Darby, he had his television-interview look on. *Committed, engaged, humble, but willing to do what's necessary*.

The Assistant Director piped up, 'We can only hope it's not *actually* Armageddon. Fukushima wasn't, in the end.'

'Not yet,' said the Chair. 'But we don't know what the fall-out – oh dear, pun *un*intended – we don't know what it'll be over the long term.'

'Well, of course, the worst fall-out is the poor Hamaoka shareholders losing all their money,' said Susan, from such an extreme height of sarcasm that normal human ears couldn't hear it. A minute later, Susan noticed the quiet woman excusing herself from the table and that was it: at 4.30am she and Graham were jarred awake by Praj on the phone, breathless, telling them a shitstorm was about to hit.

By afternoon, it had. *Susan Pike: Stock market dive "worst thing" in quake*, and *Tōkai disaster "hilarious" for Cabinet Minister's wife*. Soon came the aftershocks: a column in the *Mail*, *Who asked this prattling frump her opinion?*, and a *Times* leader, *PM must condemn these revolting comments or risk Zurich failure*. Graham and Praj met alone, and only later did they come to her, together, Praj swiping at his iPad as if clicking through worry beads.

opportunity to ensure a century of clean, sustainable energy for the world without the misguided rhetoric of scaremongers. While I emphasise again that Mrs Pike's comments in no way came from within Government, I would like to personally offer the hand of friendship to my Japanese colleagues, and reiterate that they have our ongoing support for the rescue and clean-up operation, as well as continued clean energy production now and in the future. Thank you and good afternoon.

Yukako Inoue
@kntn_yukako   6 mins
#NRS sabotage mystery deepens as US, UK, Germany, China & other pro-NR reps see "free morning" as chance to speak again

Yukako Inoue
@yukai1988   42 mins
Fever almost gone now, good I can look after by myself... Someday Prince will come, hope he is doctor :-)

KNTN Piccadilly 'office' is in fact one desk in a general media sharing company. Nick, quite handsome for an English boy, does camera and also production here for our Europe stories since four years, he says. He speaks Japanese almost well. After a 30-minute train to countryside we film a VT segment in front of the Pike house, and lots of other media are waiting under pretty flowering trees, like hanami at home. In the VT, Nick positions camera so blossom is coming in at top of the frame, very nice. The Pike house is quiet and we are leaving when suddenly voices change and phones ring all around. Twitter has **#Tōkai** trending again, and **Hamaoka** and **aftershocks** – though I don't know if this can be, when the quake is already ten days ago – and also **#tsunamiwarning**, and I make a small prayer before remembering I don't think there is any God.

No need to see TV this time. Only more pictures of lamp-posts swaying and dead grey fingers under stone, and the broken reactors filmed shaky from a distant helicopter.

I know this news is easier for reporting than Zurich, which is complicated, but I am disappointed Zurich is pushed off trending already. I search for any news on the maybe-sabotage by Nuclear Realists, while Nick leans on the trunk of a blossom tree talking Japanese on the phone. There is nothing and I put my phone away. Nick's shirt pulls up showing a line of muscle and by mistake I look. Though my ears hurt to hear his accent, I listen enough to understand he's talking to my boss. Our boss. He glances at me, then looks away. When he's finished we ride with the Sky cameras back to the station.

'Did our boss say there was a problem?' I ask Nick in English on the train.

'No no,' he says, 'he's happy. Just checking in.'
And he smiles. 'He wants us to stay with the Pike
story, keep the pressure up.'

'No Zurich report?' I ask, a little surprised.

'Ah, sort of secondary.'

But the Zurich vote is so important, maybe
the most important thing for next hundred years.
More. What if Nuclear Realists get their yes?

'Then our energy is secure for future generations,' Nick says.

There is a buzz in my ears, or in my neck, I am
not sure, and I say, 'Pardon me?'

I see him see my face. 'Oh – don't worry, I was
being ironic,' he says, which is good because to me
the NR 'secure future' looks like shaky helicopter
film.

I am glad and my neck stops buzzing. Ironic-
Nick. I smile and say in the best English, 'But who
cares for other generations when we can have
what we want for ourselves now?' but he shrugs
his shoulders so for the rest of the train journey
I am not sure whether he heard my irony or all the
meaning in what I said.

We buy train tea from the trolley, and Nick
says nothing for a small time, then asks do I like
London. It seems a small question for politeness,
but London is so big and I have been here only
seventeen hours, which I add up slowly because
I am still confused from jet lag, so I have to say I
don't know for sure, which then I am worried is
not polite for an answer. Nick laughs and says he
hopes I will learn to like it, and then birds fly up
from under my feet when he says our boss asked
on the phone if I will stay, actually for a year in
the first instance, to help make a better office for
KNTN. I touch my chest and check our boss said
me, Yukako Inoue, and Nick laughs again.

Yukako Inoue @kntn_yukako
1 hr
KNTN poll result:
UK Prime Minister apology
is enough 12%
Graham Pike should resign as
British Foreign Sec 88%

Yukako Inoue @yukai1988
45 mins
Some days this world feels very
very very big \

It feels nice to make him laugh, and I laugh too saying what-do, how-he, where-I, when-we, all bits of English tangling in a funny ball because of the very many questions in my mouth.

I stop and hold my hands up. Then I say, 'Yes, I like London,' and watch through the window, quiet, to see if it's really true. I think of my mother, push biscuit crumbs round on the table with my finger. My head and stomach like fighting kites.

There is so much future. It is not one path or two, it is more paths than we can think of, so how can I know the best? Some people speak and act so certain, but I do not know how they choose one thing or other thing, when both things could bring harm.

Graham

2020-04-05 13.40
What's going on in Z?
Antis saying sabotage

> 13.48
> I have very little idea.

13.48
Really?

> 13.49
> Really. What are
> you implying?

13.50
Just that it rather suits you
that they can't speak

13.50
You plural

Graham

14.02
The vote must be yes.
It's all that matters.

14.03
But a yes vote would
be a disaster

14.08
Better if you stay
out of it.

14.20
I take it you saw
PM's speech?

14.21
Of course, and I take it
you've heard from Praj?

Graham

14.23
Tell Praj the more he
shouts, the less likely
I am to do it. I've got
nothing to apologise for

14.24
In fact I think there's
someone else who should
be apologising. Don't you?

14.35
I give up. Do whatever you
want, Susan. But I'll tell you
something for nothing. Daisy
is very upset.

Her croaked 'Daisy?' echoes through the mobile's hollow space and she reaches to pull on the light. Graham is not in the bed. 'Are you all right?'

'Mum, I talked to Dad earlier and he says you won't listen.' Relief floods her body when she hears her daughter's voice. If she's angry, she's healthy. Unharmed, unafraid.

'Daise, it's two in the morning.'

'I know, but I can't exactly sleep. Surprised you can, actually.' There's a TV, faint, in the background.

'Dad said you were upset. I'm sorry, lovey, but it's just the media, you know you've got to ignore them.'

'It's not "just the media", Mum. It's you. You did say those things, you can't deny it.'

Susan sighs. 'I'm not denying it, sweetheart, but there are subtleties that aren't worth explaining to the press. They'll just make it up anyway.'

'*God*, you've turned into one of those "fake news" crazies!' She can hear Daisy's jaw clenched tight. 'You've got no idea what this is doing to me. I can't face anyone. That speech today...'

'Sweetie...'

'I've got ex*ams* next week.'

'I know it's hard. I do. But it's on principle, now. You didn't grow up with it: Chernobyl, *Silkwood*, nuclear-power-no-thanks. For you it was peak oil, the "energy crisis", et cetera. And they keep saying this is the easy solution, but I'm not sure it is.'

'What are you *talking* about? Oh, I get it. You know what's actually the worst thing? It's your generation that fucked this up, used all the fossil fuels, and now you're saying that for the future, that's *my* future, Mum, you're not going to let us have nuclear either, which by the way is *safe*, statistically, and it's totally low-carbon, the original sustainable energy?'

'Daisy–'

'We've *got* to do this. They vote yes, we go to 80% nuclear worldwide, and we *actually* have a future, so why don't you let us worry about the details? It's called Nuclear Realism for a reason, you know.'

'This is for you, Daisy,' is all she can say.

'Oh *please.*'

There's a tiny beep in her ear. A BBC news app alert. Zurich.

'Mum. Just do the apology.'

'Turn up the TV,' she says, and scrabbles for the remote.

I arrive at press conference early, check the new batteries in the Sony recorder, put my phone on silent. Still no answer from my mother. I have the strange feeling, like time is short, though Hajime says she is fine, so I try to turn my mind to work instead. There is one woman here already, with black and white glasses, in the front row, as if she is there since last night. I sit three rows back but Nick has to stand to the side because he is filming. In spite of worry for my mother I feel a lightness, I think because media have kept the pressure and now Mrs Pike is going to speak at last. Somehow I feel not so lonesome.

When Praj puts his smug shiny head round the door, Susan doesn't turn. 'Looking like a full house,' he says. Then his voice goes sugary. 'You're doing the right thing, Susie. For Graham, for the party. For yourself. For the world! I know how important that is to you.'

She focuses on her notes.

The advisor I've seen before, speaking for the Minister, comes to podium and makes us quiet with his eyes. He is a bald man with oil on his face. 'Hello, boys and girls,' he says. I look quickly to Nick and he looks to me at same time, which makes me make a tiny smile myself when I look away. 'We'll be kicking off in just a few moments, if we can get ourselves ready?'

Susan Pike walks to the podium and coughs quietly into her hand. She glances at the assembled faces.

'Ladies and Gentlemen, thank you for coming today. This has been a very difficult few days for me and my family, though of course not in comparison with the suffering of the innocent victims of the Tōkai and the subsequent crisis at Hamaoka, which is still of critical concern, not only in Japan but everywhere in the world.

'I am here today to apologise unreservedly for the offence caused by the reporting of certain words I spoke last Friday at a private charity event.'

I am hoping the Sony will pick up the speech okay with the flash cameras going loud, like teeth crunching. The eyes of Mrs Pike are big and brown and wet.

'I would emphasise that the meaning given to my words after the event was not in any way the meaning I intended. In fact, it was quite the opposite.'

Susan swallows and turns a page.

'Now that we know the outcome of the so-called Nuclear Realism vote in Zurich, I'd like to not only apologise for the offence, but to state quite clearly that I am ha-

'That I am ha-'

She stops to stare in the corner for a long time, twenty seconds, like her Event Failed.

'A-hem, that I am heartbroken, about Hamaoka, about the earthquake, about the yes vote and about all disasters present and future, natural and man-made. May our daughters, and our sons, and our mothers and fathers for that matter, forgive us for what we are doing.'

I wonder if others here have noticed – but maybe not as they are typing on phones and making shorthand scribbling – but her face has come to change.

'And I am also sorry to announce, ladies and gentlemen, that my marriage of twenty-seven years has come to an end. But my husband instructed me recently to look into my conscience, and that I have done. Perhaps you might, yourselves, look into the sabotage at the summit in Zurich, and at my husband's interests. Thank you.'

There are shouts and excitement, like a movie, and I call out Mrs Pike Mrs Pike like the rest, but if they point for me to ask a question I don't know what it will be. Then she leaves anyway, taking no questions, and soon the media end filming VTs and go away to file. Nick is in a corner, reviewing tape.

I switch my phone back from silent and see one new email. My mother. Next I am in Ladies and sitting on a closed seat, reading. Words keep swelling like a fish-eye lens and I must blink. *My dear Yukako, she writes, it is time for forgiving. We have made each other so lonely...*

Yes good afternoon Fiona and thanks, I'm here outside Westminster as you can see behind me where the media are coming out after Susan Pike's statement, a lot of media interest of course and there will be a lot of reaction now, as just a few moments ago Mrs Pike left after her apology, or what many of us thought was going to *be* an apology, but in fact what has just happened here, in the building behind me here, is that she has *doubled down* on her original position by distancing herself quite extraordi*nari*ly from her husband's Nuclear Realist, from his position on Nuclear Realism, which as you will know has become clear as being very strongly in favour of the proposals being put forward in Zurich this week, the 80% global 2050 target. Mrs Pike even went so far as to make the suggestion that Graham Pike could have in some way been involved... erm... involved in... oh, Fiona, I don't know if you can see here, perhaps if I move to one side, here, excuse me

I stay a while in there, sitting and reading and starting to make a reply and not knowing what to say to start with when there is so much to choose from. I start to worry that Nick must think I have left, so I try to get my breaths to come to normal but it doesn't come to normal as quickly as I want. Soon I hear coughing, and shoes clipping-clopping louder, until the door of the Ladies opens up. Then it seems the door lock on my cubicle was only pretending that it worked, and it is Susan Pike pushing the door open towards my knees and I look in the brown wet eyes and she looks in mine.

'Oh! Sorry,' she says and at same time I say, 'Sorry, sorry, no,' and push the door back closed.

I hear her pee and cough and sigh and swear very quiet. Messages blip to her phone, and I hear her tick-tack reply typing and she is sniffing, and finally she is shuffling clothes and coming out. I wait for her leaving but she stands for minutes with water falling at the washbasin. So I come out. She still types on the phone. Then she looks at me using the wall mirror instead of straight, as if we are two less real people, which is maybe the reason she feels okay to not pretend it is all fine.

She holds up her phone and shrugs shoulders. 'My daughter,' she says, and gives me a smile like December sun. 'We don't always understand each other.'

I can see she is thinking I am the same as her daughter because I look young, and probably because I have been crying. Though I am nearly ten years older than her daughter, who has the name Daisy Pike – which I asked Nick if everyone laughs at the name, because it sounds to me funny that a fish and a flower are together, or whether it seems normal to English. He said he hadn't noticed but that now I said it, it did seem funny to him, but also that parents don't always think what they are giving to their children, probably English parents no worse than others, but he didn't know.

So she is looking at me and thinking about her daughter, and I am looking at her knowing she is a stranger and we are both professional, but also remembering that inside my phone in my bag my mother has just reached out her arms for me from 10,000km away, and here is this woman who is a mother too. It's nice feeling, and even though in a way we are using each other for to feel better, it is fine because we are both doing right, or as right as we can know. Something we can stand by because we think others must harm less this way.

She says 'I'm –' but then her eyebrows shoot close together and she starts to cough, a deep hard coughing into paper tissue.

'Here.' I look in my handbag and hold out cough sweet, an excellent Japanese throat soothing lozenge. 'Taste like honey.'

Yes I'm sorry Fiona, it's a little, *ha*, a little chaotic here at the moment as I think... some... protesters may be trying to... excuse me, if we move... yes, I don't know if you can see at home in the picture but there are some quite vehement members... members of the public who have joined the circus of, the circle of the media here outside Westminster even though security... we did come through quite a tight security border, a barrier that we had to come through earlier into this special area that we... but here they are and I have to say they *seem* peaceful in spite of, ha, in spite of the noise that you can hear... sorry, if we could just move... and it looks as if they are actually in support of Mrs Pike, in support... or certainly protesting against *Graham* Pike, the Foreign Minister, himself, quite personally in some of the... on some of the placards here. So that implies I suppose that they will be supporting Susan Pike *de facto* as it were, as she has just quite unprecedently made the surprise and very personal announcement about her marriage *to* the Minister, and as I say also those very unexpected comments about the sabotage, the alleged sabotage at the Zurich summit, which as you know are allegations that some of the voices opposing the Zurich motion were unable to speak because of what the organisers have said were technical problems, but which the anti-Nuclear Realist lobby are still maintaining was

a type of sabotage of their, of
their, equipment, of laptops and
materials gone missing. Which
of course I should stress are *just*
allegations, nothing more than
that, and certainly there is no
evidence or no suggestion that
Graham Pike, other than his wife's
allegation just now – sorry – no
suggestion that the Minister had
anything to do with any alleged
involvement, though some will
say his particular business links
do give him – sorry – yes – sorry
Fiona, I've been told we're very
much out of time, back to you.

ELIMINATE TOXINS AND
INCREASE BLOOD FLOW

Tuesday comes round so quick. I'm on reception, sneaking Jaffa Cakes and fidgeting at my uniform, the trousers riding up tight. The top keeps gaping, too; these last few weeks I've been constantly tugging it closed. I must be washing them too hot.

I've just finished the packet of Jaffa Cakes when in he comes.

'Hello, Lindsey.'

We get a lot of regulars at Sabai Sabai. The stressed, the knotted-up, the office worker treating herself because she's worth it. We're clean, the atmosphere's the whole jasmine, nag champa, gamelan music thing, and we're not expensive. We do offer threading and pedicures, all of that, but it's mostly your traditional Thai massage. I went on the course when too much Swedish gave me RSI, and started here after one of the real Thai girls got deported.

With Thai, you do use your hands, but you use your elbows too, and your feet. As long as the client's up for it, we'll walk on them – there are these wooden bars on the wall up by the ceiling that we hold on to – it gives us that extra pressure for when back muscles really resist.

The other girls are all lovely. 'English in body, Thai in heart,' Kha says, nodding and pointing at my chest. We look out for each other like sisters, and they're always giving me chocolates and cakes they don't want. On the whole, it's a nice place to work.

But I hate Tuesdays. Tuesdays are when Mr Smeed comes in.

He's a white slug. Skin like rice paper, flesh like jelly underneath, as if he's spent his whole life on a damp mattress in a cellar, eating margarine. At his first three appointments he asked whether we did extras. 'To completion,' he called it. Usually we warn once and then it's zero-tolerance, but he got away with it until I mentioned it on Kha's hen night and it turned out he'd tried it with three of us in turn. Now he knows not to ask for extras when he comes in, every Tuesday. But he always asks for me.

Every time he comes in he says, 'Hello, Lindsey.'

It's the way he says it.

I show him to the Lotus Room, let him undress and settle with his face in the hole and a towel over him, and take a few slow breaths before I go in.

I oil my hands and get going on his calves. His calf and gastroc muscles are thick and stodgy.

'How's that pressure for you?' is the question we have to ask.

'That's lovely, Lindsey,' says Mr Smeed, as always.

I move up to his thighs and focus on my breathing for

five cellulite-filled minutes. When the thighs are done, I pull the towel down over them, baring his back. The pocked skin is thinly strewn with hairs, like some sick sea bed after a chemical spill. I sweep the area, up-down, up-down, and the flesh ripples under my thumbs.

'Mmmm,' he says into the hole.

Now I clamber onto the edges of the table, grab the wall bars and place a foot on his lower back.

'Ooof,' he says. 'Mmmm.'

Drool hits the floor under his face. I lift my weight and rest the other foot in his soft mid-back.

'Urgh. Mmmm. You can go harder, Lindsey, if you like.'

OK.

I'm still holding on to the wall bars, but I let some weight down through my heels and rock slightly, transferring the pressure either side of the spine. I step along gradually, away from the dough of his buttocks. Mr Smeed gurgles like a blocked drain.

Then – I don't know why; maybe I feel like I could balance better, maybe I want to rest my arms, maybe I just feel encouraged to do it – I let go of the bars.

He squeals: a wheezing yelp of shock, like a dog hit by a lorry. There's another sound, too, a sudden wet squidge. The bursting of a meat balloon.

Then it's quiet.

For a few moments, I freeze. Instead of his papery skin, it's the table I feel, solid, under my feet. I've gone straight through. I reach for the bars again even though it's too late. Holding on, I don't look down, already knowing the awful thing I'd see from the hot, slippery mess I'm up to my ankles in. I don't panic, though. I just call out for Kha, who comes in, stops for a second, says, 'Okay,' and takes hold of my hands to help me down.

Of course, there are consequences. We close for half a day with a note on the door saying *Sorry! Staff Training*. Everyone rallies round – methodical, wordless, quick. We are glad of our clinical waste licence: the lorry comes twice a week and those yellow hazard bags don't exactly make you want to look inside.

The girls are great about what happened. In fact, they bring me a sandwich every day now, as well as chocolate biscuits twice a week. 'Is good for you,' says Kha, with that quick nod she has. 'Good for all of us.'

BIOPHILE

—I'm down maybe five feet. Muslin over my mouth and nose. I take a moment to thank the leaf-filled rectangle of sky, yank the tarpaulin, and the black mound falls. Then I pull the tarp out of the way and scrunch it down my side, and delicious hunks and crumbles of dug earth say: welcome.

I allow a last minute of earthly thought and congratulate myself on this ingenious arrangement. The spot in the forest, far from anywhere. The tarp and the spade. The digging – a long hole, deep enough to work, deep enough to be right – and the piling of the soil on the tarp with a good strip hanging over for easy tugging. The hurried discard of clothes, my body a chilly worm. It gets warm as you go down: a reminder you're entering a living thing.

Here's the idea. Lie here, breathing with care, and make a long, long count to five in the glorious black. See what happens. At some point my wish will come true and I'll bud; a tendril will burst from me in spite of it all, wrap me into the world. From my flat edges, roundness.

In time, I'll push up and out into the mossy night. Ejected from under the skin of the world, I'll be real again, greener, humming with mitochondria. A twig in the nest, a bee in the hive, a member of the family, a body in a body-shaped space—

At my desk, in the anti-tanning glow of my monitor, I was clicking. Clicking, clicking. I'd had no three-toadstools/soft-porn-fairy yet that day, but from spin to spin I'd got a decent number of gnarled oaks and weeping willows appearing on paylines, even one five of a kind. Only Qs, but those five Qs brought me even. I took my hand off the mouse and had a celebratory drink. And I had a celebratory jelly snake from the top desk drawer.

I noted rhythmic splashes outside, so I bent and twisted to raise the blind for a little dose.

From the low window of my attic office I could get a clear if uncomfortable view of the pool. Craig was bombing the deep end and I watched Stephen pull himself out of the water, stretching as he stood. How he had grown. Speedo, dark line running down towards. I crossed my legs the other way. On the one hand, he was still a teenager and I was his thirty-nine-year-old aunt. On the other: no actual blood relation, so.

I sat up, clicked, clicked again.

On Enchanted Forest time sank away with a sigh. My skull grew a sweet new lining as my finger clicked Spin. The reels fell with that jaunty bounce: 1, 2, 3, 4, 5. Over and over.

Doink doink doink doink doink.

An email came from Funsoft. Feedback from Animation: a little more saturation in the colours, please, and they needed me to knock up a quick moorland for the background, if I didn't mind. With the email came a twinge. If they knew I was on a PlayHouse game? On work time?

I clicked away, spun again. Work time was flexitime. And I needed to see those toadstools.

I liked to start with 500 credits. Though one credit equalled one actual pound sterling in some universe – like, our in-lieu-of-any-kind-of-pension, savings-account universe – it wasn't a universe I wanted to deal with while I was playing. Thanks, but no thanks. In that same realm I was hollow with hunger, my bladder a hot balloon of pain – but it was good/painful, painful/good. I was held still, light, like being inside a meringue cooling on a marble surface in an empty kitchen. At peace with my dead parents, my defunct ovaries, in the smooth flat world of 1, 2, 3, 4, 5.

Spap. A Skype-chat message: it was Warren, on his laptop in the living room.

World calling Danielle... Coming down? :-)

A pause. *Spap.*

Friday night drinks & nibbles being served... A&P doing dinner...

Lovely Warren. His cosy Skype-chat tone, the winks and ellipses and ampersands, the entreaties to come down: all designed to lever me from my chair. Warren and my office chair were sexual rivals; he admitted as much during the one actual row we'd had since we moved. Otherwise, we coexisted fine – me and my loose ways, him and his straight, clean mildness. If I thought about Warren I sort of zoomed in and out on him, like one of those macro pictures made of smaller pictures, that softens as you pull away and reveals its detail when you get close. I bet if we'd ended up having kids together I'd have had my nose pressed to that detail every day. So, probably, it was for the best.

Be right down! Just finishing off! <enter>

Pause.

X <enter>

He always noticed when I left off the X, and would distance himself to a certain smooth resolution which he thought was a punishment. But I didn't want to stir things up, not with his family here.

—Ears lost in the silence. Eyes numb in the dark.

Bliss.

But oh. There's a niggle. A bother.

It was that thanking the sky thing: it's a habit from my parents. Doing that, bringing them into it, I've gone a bit... I mean, I can breathe okay – there's plenty of air when the earth's well-dug – but I think, oh, I do, I feel quite sick. And I'm on my back. I didn't plan for that.

I'm nauseated from the whole rollercoaster weekend. Everything I was keeping calm, now broken up and churning. Trying not to think about it makes me think about it, and thinking makes me want to actually vomit, as I lie here—

A text came to my phone and I ignored it. Spin. Doink doink doink doink doink. Okay, nice, four fluffy bunnies, and I'm actually up by five credits. Maybe stop there? But downstairs there was food to negotiate. People. One more click. Here was one toadstool, two toadstools, and…?

We had to admire PlayHouse: their games owned you. Enchanted Forest was a 20-line slot I'd had to try out for work, and three months later I was still trying it out. Daily. It was nothing groundbreaking: three rows and five reels with a standard 10-J-Q-K-A base, plus the required set of icons, the little squares of metonymy that illustrate the theme. Saucy Bambis were the best five-of-a-kinds, winning you 5,000 virtual 10p coins, but you really kept spinning for three toadstools boinging into place on reels 1, 3 and 5. These start a bonus round where you mouse a sort of soft-porn-fairy over flowers to "pick" them for their hidden prize, the reward climbing and climbing – just how good might this *get?* – until you hit one that turns into a dandelion clock which blows itself out and frightens the soft-porn-fairy away and that's it, back you go to the pregnant Spin button, and during that time the planet drops out of the galaxy and you seem to have no heartbeat, though something must be forcing those martinis of adrenalin and dopamine through the scrawled lines of your system.

No. No third toadstool, not this time and not the last eight times, so surely soon? Dull, dull, stupid, stupid Enchanted Forest. Maybe switch to Underwater Adventure? Those little dolphins can make your day.

The light had softened. I bent to raise the blind: yes, the sun was way down, the tops of the pines spiking the pool with shadow. Stephen lay on a lounger on his front, reading. My eyes licked the length of the long dip that marked his spine.

Warren's brother Paul and beautiful Antonia and their boys were here one more week. I wasn't used to having people physically present for a whole fortnight. With Warren's family there was the benefit of Stephen, but the trade-off was Paul.

Everyone liked to visit since we moved to this village idyll. So pretty! We were so lucky – on holiday all the time! Except even if you're retired, which we were nothing like, you can't be on holiday all the time. Stay anywhere more than three weeks and you have to face things as they really are. The washing machine breaks down and the plumber rants unprompted for ten minutes about 'les noirs'. The post goes on strike. When the wind blows from the east there's a smell of rotted meat. You witness, one day, what looks like a puppy being thrown from a moving car. So you retreat to your cool office which with the blinds down could be anywhere, and skulk over to the expat shop, pay twelve euros for Marmite.

They're not really boys, though. It's strange and sort of miraculous. Last time I saw them, back in England, they were children, and Craig at thirteen still was. Throaty, self-conscious Craig, fists in the air with each tiny triumph over his brother. A nice kid, but his father's son and, thankfully, forgettable. But Stephen, you wouldn't believe. How had Stephen, 6'2", clear eyes like truffles, skin of toasted hazelnut, grown into this tranquil masculinity that he wore like a tux? How did he know *how*?

A sudden *bloop-de-bloop*! made me drop the blind with a clatter.

Funsoft Office calling: *Answer with video?*

Hm. O'Really would know it was nearly seven here. I minimised the game and answered, and my boss's moustached head filled the monitor. In the corner window my own face darted, tiny and pale, like a guilty haricot bean.

'OK: nightmare,' said O'Really. 'It's a no from the Brontë people.'

'Shit. So. Plan B?'

'Sign-off by closework Monday. Sorry, Danni.'

My mobile buzzed. Paul, texting me from the downstairs loo. My rule was to ignore one in three of his texts and I ignored this one.

'Can we keep the creaking gate?' I asked O'Really. 'And the sheep?'

'They can stay. Better change the interfering house-keeper, though, she's too obviously Nelly Dean. Maybe make her a sexy maid? Nice weekend.'

We rang off and I messaged Warren.

Work just sent more work! Enough for whole weekend!! :-(Down soon. <enter>

X <enter>

O'Really – because he never believes what you say you've been doing all day – had been reluctant to let me (as he put it) quotes-work-from-home when Airbus moved Warren to Toulouse. To show him, I'd finished three new games in the last year. We were becoming contenders: manage-ment thought our new literary slots would out-sophisticate PlayHouse. I didn't think so, but they were a rich seam of symbols for us designers. Our most popular lit so far was the title 1984tune!, for which I'd drawn a grim, grey-jawed Winston and domestic-but-hot Julia. I'd storyboarded the whole bonus round: you released rats into Winston's prison-cage, where he screamed and rattled the bars, and with each rat your prize increased, until – jeopardy! – you released one too many, Winston fainted, and you lost half your total. So there was an element of control/risk. Players loved that.

Funsoft's internal slogan was simple: Keep Players Playing. Which meant: get people addicted. Seduce them, blanket them with snuggly narcotic sensations. Get them to bury themselves in your two bright dimensions of zipping video candy.

The lits brought some estate-reputation issues, and Plan B on Wuthering Heights meant a total remodel, fraught with the pangs of artistic compromise – Blustering Crags, we'd call it, with new character names, visuals nudged just far enough away from the originals to keep the estate lawyers at bay. I fired up Photoshop to tinker with the new Wycliffe and Kitty. In my little blinds-drawn attic, a thousand miles from O'Really, I worked with eyebrows raised, a tilt to my head, expressing my distaste for the task.

In this way, from my chair, I rebelled.

—My chin's going tight. Trying to move just stirs up the *ugh*. With an empty stomach you can't actually *be* sick, can you? The icons of Prize Picnic whirl by: a helter-skelter ice cream; a cupcake's cherry nipple; the plump bronze curves of roast poultry. Or can you? There's always bile. Oh God. I see little square pictures of my mouth bubbling yellow, my eyes wide with choke.

I hear their voices: *Harmony Meadow, lie still. Shush, now.*

I hear Warren: *Christ, Danni, what were you thinking?*

The soil's heavy, heavier than I thought. I tug at a crease in the tarpaulin but it stretches, comes to tearing point. My heart flags up the growing trouble—

I'd been good, really working for a full half hour, and when I stretched I noticed it was dark. I heard Warren's feet on the wood of the stairs. Quick, I had to make sure nothing from Paul was visible in email and where was my phone? In the drawer: okay. I x-ed out of Photoshop and in my hurry clicked *No* to *Save changes?* because I was thinking *No* to Warren's footsteps. Shit, thanks so much Warren, who was now pushing open the door with the gentle nudge of a PlayHouse doe.

'Hi.'

It was Stephen. Oh Stephen, suddenly fleshing out the room. I felt twin compulsions: a) to cover myself like a nun, b) to rip off everything.

'Hi.'

'We were wondering if you're coming down?'

'Course!'

I was already rising from my chair.

—I'm sorry if you're getting queasy too, all this spinning, and zooming in and out, bending and straightening and getting up off chairs, and raising and lowering blinds. All the indulgent oversaturated description. It's not everyone's idea of a good time, I know. I feel pretty awful too.

It's disgust that's making me tight and green and bilious. Down here my body's still; I mean, nothing's swinging, revolving or swooping, but oh, those internal oscillations: boom-boom, flush-flush, boom-boom, flush-flush—

As the relentless dinner progressed, Craig begged for a second half-glass of beer and I went inside and stuck my head in the drinks fridge. Five moments passed, steady, each a degree cooler than the one before as my personal universe expanded. Then – *oh* – Stephen was behind me, his deep, woody scent stirring my insides. My spine pulled into a spiked pelt of longing; the world blew, bellowed, into throbbing 3D. I passed him beers, noted the strong curve of his hand grasping the shaft of each bottle. I would not think about this later. I would not think about it ever. No way would I mess everything up by acting on this.

I followed him out. Cicadas or crickets or whatever scraped the air to shreds. Stephen bent to relight the citronella coils and as I tried not to look, I noticed that beside their lemony tang there was a sort of emotional smoke in the air. In my absence, there had been talk. As I sat down, everyone else's movements slowed and stopped, dropping into place: 1, 2, 3, 4, 5.

At the end of the table, glowing in her white linen shirt in the candlelight, beautiful Antonia rested her glass.

'Danielle honey, we want to talk to you.'

'You have been talking to me.'

'Danni –'

Paul reached over and almost touched my hand, stopping at the last centimetre. 'It's good to see you, D.'

'We want you back,' Warren said, staring at his empty plate.

'This is because we care about you.'

Then it clicked: everyone looking at me? The quiet that had fallen over the remains of dinner? This was one of those whatchamacallits. An intervention.

'We miss you,' said Warren. 'I miss you.'

His family all turned away, giving us a notional moment alone in the chirruping dark.

'Um.'

I'd made a mistake somewhere. Which one of the axes I juggled had hacked this sudden sickening gash into my day? Things could have been uncovered, correspondence opened, activities come to light. They all watched the tilt of my wine-pouring wrist.

'OK. Well. So, what do you want?'

'What do you mean?'

'What is it you think's wrong with me?'

They were all staring, all five of them, like how can you not know?

Then Antonia counted off on her long fingers.

'The starving yourself, my love. The working all day and all night, or whatever you do in there. The drinking. The endless quipping, not being straight, talking in riddles. Sweetie. The *avoiding*.'

At least there were no specifics: no names, no numbers. Maybe they hadn't seen right into me, not yet.

'I mean. I don't *starve*. I had a huge salad for lunch –'

'Salad's not food, D.'

'And I eat sweets all the time. You know I like those jelly snakes.'

I didn't like my thin voice. Warren, quiet, said it all had to change, and I said sorry, then I said it again differently – sometimes you try a few keys in the door before you find the one that fits. But Antonia kept pressing, batting away my responses. It was like being the kid the other kids turn on in a snowball fight, then realising your favourite teacher told them to do it.

Antonia overflowed with lucky loveliness: her velvet dark-brown skin and firm convex body came from jackpot Cuban/Guyanese genes. She'd earned two international postgrad degrees, and since having the boys she'd become so tender, so solid. Paul – a puffier, louder version of Warren – seemed blind to his incredible good fortune, flirting in emails, indulging in the soft types of eye contact, leaning too close to people who weren't Antonia. Maybe his obliviousness kept her attracted. Maybe she was just a Good Faithful Person.

Stephen elbow-dug his brother for doing an under-table phone check. Was he on my side? I wanted to ask him out loud, but, Danielle, sanity.

I said okay. I'd do better, I'd change, stop drinking, stop, whatever, letting them all down. For proof I chewed a hearty chunk of bread.

Then Warren said, 'What about the chickens?'

Everyone looked at him.

'We were going to do a little smallholding, chickens and stuff; she was supposed to look into it and start it off, get the eggs or whatever.'

Paul said, 'I don't think you get chickens from eggs.' Everyone looked at him.

'You know what I mean.'

I swallowed. 'Okay,' I said again. 'We'll talk details, but fine.'

Antonia said, 'If you mean it, you'll do morning yoga with me.'

I could see she was aware of the way the candlelight bounced off the taut skin of her arms.

'Yoga?' I said, 'I mean, I don't even. I don't do that stuff.'

A yoga-themed *game?* Yes. Why hadn't we done one already? PlayHouse hadn't. I could see the reels: 1, 2, 3, 4, 5, all bendy limbs and primary leotards. But not just people in poses, you have to differentiate your icons: the clarity increases player speed. Maybe turn the metaphors back on themselves, have a real downward-facing dog, a real cobra. Spinning, I don't know, locusts. Well, it would need work.

'*Something* physical then, darling. You have to do something for your body.'

I nodded yes to Antonia, gripped Warren's out-held hand. Noted Paul's gaze, full of thoughts of *body* directed at me like fleshy darts. I tucked it away, perhaps a last indulgence to sink into, pathetic though it was.

The boys felt an unspoken permission granted and picked up their forks again, and I smiled at Warren and made sure I kept smiling until the tableau melted back into the evening they all wanted. I let them relax, each one believing I was still there with them at the table. Smiling, above ground, happy and calm under their corrective gaze.

—No, no, no, no, no. Soil's crept in now, under the muslin. I try to downsnort like a horse but it won't move. The swirling poison rises to my throat. Why are we stuck, you and me both? This is madness.

I gain a tiny edge by pushing down through my calves. Damp disks crush my eyes through the lids, cool coins of the dead, as my face levers up. I'm sure I'm going to throw up. I shouldn't have dug the hole so deep; I should have known I'm made for elsewhere, I'm no worm. I should have considered the sheer weight of the soil.

But no, I have to think of it as not-weight,
weightless. The soil is an illusion—

Five miles from home, soft sandy path under my boots,
I took a taste of newness onto my tongue. Doves sat three
feet overhead and watched as I passed. A hairy railway of
processional caterpillars chugged along unbothered. The
air like mint. All right, I did feel better. And they would all
be at home feeling better about me, out for a health-giving
Saturday morning walk.

I felt better and better, actually, and the betterness soon
got sharp and high-pitched. Surrounded by four thousand
square miles of forest I wanted to go on a rampage, to crunch
through it all like a giant. To snap it into twigs, twiglets, and
shovel them into my mouth with a fist, get that chlorophyll
blast of life into my flesh. It had been so long since once
upon a time. The sap bolstering the blood, the humming
mushroom mulch of the forest floor plumping up my liver
and lungs.

I wrapped my limbs around a fatherly beech and clung
there like a primate. The PlayHouse elephants in Zany Zoo
(1,000 coins for five) have long eyelashes, a slutty smirk.
Players will lap up flirtation from no matter where. I gripped
tighter, thinking I might crack, sprout something from my
solar plexus or between my legs, vibing with the hopeful
hum of the tree.

I'd meant all my promises last night. From now on, things
would be clean and healthy: they'd see I could let it all go, no
problem. I'd have a month, three months, with no drinking or
sweets or extracurricular game playing and when I got a stab
of hunger I'd eat something. Something with butter on it, and

I'd work only my contracted hours, and no weekends. A life like a smooth white stone. It was fine! I still had my little attic room, the dropping squares and rhythms of my work and my thoughts. The swing of deprivation and indulgence I was riding – too much, too far, too much, too far – I'd simply step off.

I couldn't hang on to the tree for long. I walked on.

Their loving inquisition was for my sake, to help me live better. It made sense in the same way my parents made sense of what they did to us. It must have rather hurt them, my gentle parents, who were not at all dead as far as I knew, but farming quietly into their old age, chickens and all, somewhere near Totnes. It must have hurt them to hear their children whimpering and begging to be dug out, to have to walk away and leave us until morning.

The burial ritual was for the benefit of all beings, and we would benefit most, though we were soft and small, and frightened. Our knowledge of suffering would increase, and so in turn would our compassion, which would ripple out to the world. My mother may have put it in those terms in her last letter, but I only skim-read it before throwing it away. Maybe she said we needed to be inoculated against the corrupting ego. There was definitely a phrase about stimulating the sympathetic response – one of their homeopathy concepts – and how the ceremony was a kind of *memento mori*, the lesson being that not only does everyone suffer, but everything ends in death.

An unforgettable lesson for seven-year-old Harmony Meadow Daniels. I ditched HM finally at sixteen, salvaging only the scrap of surname as I gathered myself up and ran for adulthood. I left my younger siblings behind. After all, the older ones had left me.

And I still didn't blame my parents.

I stopped to pee, stepping off the path to squat. As I darkened the sand I looked up at the forest canopy in all innocence. It went so high, branch after branch after branch. Such a lot of leaves – how many millions, how many billions, all pushing to come out each year, pressing, breathing, flicking with the wind and tipping as the rain rolls off, up there day after day with no one to see? How many billions falling and crumbling and then more billions coming above, again and again?

All at once the trees were overwhelmingly massive, just too numbersome, about to collapse on top of me. I ducked, still squatting, and nearly toppled. I mustn't fall, but I couldn't stand – there was no good direction to go in. Like a frantic fly hammering a window, I had to get out.

But I was already *out*.

I would survive if I got back to my desk. For comfort, I pictured home, but the picture was the House of Usher in a swirl of choking mist, due to last night's dinner: the ripping away of all my compensations, my consolations. Two doves fluttered up and bumped chests overhead and then my knees went, I buckled to the sand, and I was down on my hands and haunches with my clothes still round my ankles, wracked by the Hole.

The Hole won't take the honest flesh of a decent name. It's just the Hole. But it's the reason for our sickening excess of words, for my mind's endless, heinous, lies. For my badly directed desires, my failures to be Good. The reason for the habits of an empty girl.

Broken pinecones dug into my knees and a slick of drool spinneyed to the ground under my melting face. I coughed out my own name, insisting, *Danielle*, still running from that other girl. Leaning my two hard fists on pine-needley sand felt good/painful, painful/good. Maybe this was what it meant to be alive.

If so, well. Thanks, but no thanks.

I wrestled my clothes up and semi-stood.

Turned to the forest, I faced spikes of acacia and piney brush which fell over each other in a way that looked designed, enticing. I let them lead me through to a flat, clear-ish spot, and dragged over some fallen branches. With some scrabbling the sandy clods of ground came away, and soon I had a shallowing I could lie down in, scuff-brushing the loosened soil and leafy branches over me as best I could. It was too bright, too gay with birds, but what could I do.

Then, closed eyes and stillness. Slow breaths coming. There would soon come a tipping point: surely I would shoot, germinate, in spite of it all. I just needed to keep at it. After a few minutes I touched myself, and maybe it wasn't me doing it, maybe it was an outside force. My mind didn't care, and though there were thoughts of Stephen the signal was weak, the data corrupted, and it all got outflooded by some savagery of the forest itself sinking its jaws into the scruff of my neck and I let go.

And after all that, it wasn't enough. It was good and everything, but I was unfulfilled. In time I brushed off my walking clothes and set off for home, slightly ashamed to be upright, as if I was over-evolved.

Then, that night, after dinner, everything got messy.

—The soil is an illusion. Not matter, but a dream. In this way mountains can be moved. See, Harmony? You can move a mountain. Shitshitshit I am under a mountain

No. Calm. Breathe. Don't be sick.

Breathe just a bit. It's all I need. I chose this. I am all-powerful. I am the universe. I could do a game based on the gods. A game based on consciousness itself.

No, forget the games. Fuck them.

I wriggle a finger and feel the earth settle tighter around my hand. I veer from stabs of hope to the soft murmurs of submission, the hope worse than the fear.

Then no, no, yes, this is it, here it comes, the eruption—

Dinner over, everyone else elsewhere. In the night quiet we stood among the trees behind the house, breathing. An owl yelped above us, right overhead, as if it knew.

'Let's not do this,' Paul said.

I tidied my hair and reset my straps, giving Paul five minutes' grace to get back into the house. I was thinking of a new game: bankers? Bailouts? He'd said something over dinner about financial instruments, so now I saw a marching band of money: euro tubas, coin-topped snare drums. But it fizzled out. I used to be able to entertain myself with this stuff. Now things had finally taken a turn for the three-dimensional with Paul, it had lost its taste.

Back in the cool dark of the garden, I perched on a lounger, watching the moonless night ruffle the pool, tapping musky fingers against my lips. Paul's six-month pursuit by text and email, my six months of coy-mistressing, come to this: a sad, sober grope on an after-dinner tryst. Kissing that began with mutual interest but fell out of sync. My hands in the dark hoped for a touch of the son, found only the fluorescent pudge of the father. Yet it wasn't me who'd stopped it.

I lay back, imagining how it would be to stay out all night, exposed to nipping insects and the awful eyes of the stars.

Twelve hours later Sunday lunch undid me. I thought to offer Stephen lamb from my fork, his harmless aunt with too much on her plate, and instead some unfathomable stupidity left over from the excess stupidity of the night before made me hold it out to Paul, touching it almost to his lips. Warren froze, caught my eye, then looked as if the cells of his face were crumbling. Beautiful Antonia saw everything, looked at her plate and did a tiny shake of her head. And I, worm, welcomed that spark of victory fizzing in my guts.

But the boys saw too.

I crept to the stairs in the post-lunch slump. Heading for my attic I paused with a foot raised, and overheard:

'You'd better not just, like, forgive him.'

'There's nothing to forgive, darling. We mustn't jump to conclusions.'

'Yeah, right.'

'Even if they... No one was trying to hurt you.'

'I don't even get it. She's not even nice looking.'

'Now, come on, Stephen.'

Silence.

'Don't cry, lovey.'

I couldn't climb the stairs. Down was the only way for me. Down was an okay dimension now. That's when the plan dropped into place: note, spade, woods, pit, root.

It's been three days. Her boss has flown over, saying Funsoft is frantic about her, though Warren suspects the panic is mainly to do with her unfinished work. But to be fair, O'Reilly seems like a decent man. Chunky. Fills a room. Warren wishes O'Reilly had stayed with them instead of opting for the run-down hotel in the square – having an outsider like him in the house might have kept the situation urgent for the others. The boys have sunk into their gadgets, Paul keeps making tea, and in her elegant, un-narcissistic way, Antonia is blaming herself. None of them can help with Danni's infuriating one-line note.

When the police come they act like friends, taking black coffee and smoking freely in the garden. But friends who might turn. Warren tingles with the awareness that he must act as the innocent he is, which makes him do many things he wouldn't normally do. Then he corrects those things, which makes him seem inconsistent, and in quiet moments he feels he may be dissolving, becoming a kind of mirrored mirror image of himself.

They used to pass each other in the rooms of their home, exchanging spaces like a weatherhouse couple. Though his wife was tiny she was his ballast. With her compulsions and evasions, her bloody insistence on living through symbols and metaphors instead of facing reality, they counterbalanced. Now, without her, he swings and swoops, a horrible pendulum.

> —I feel it go, pushing through the back of my left knee, slightly sickening yes but already so natural, thin as candlewick but strong, rooting down, finding its way blindly through the complex of grit and black and the cool webs of fibre and the first hints of the heat of the heart of the earth. It tapers to a stop. For

the next hours it will swell, pressing the knee open, open, more open, until a pivot point when I let go and give in and allow the knee to split completely and stop being a knee. You're free to go. And at that moment there's the sweetest relief—

FLAMINGO LAND

This Procedure Unit was one of the okay ones, ish – the big stained concrete building might once have been a real hospital. I knew the best place to park because it was right behind the FHO where we went for Assessment.

I scraped the dirty slush off my trainers, went in and gave Mum's name, and they sent me up to the third floor. I found her near the end of the ward, half-propped on a bottom bunk, looking at an old *Gourmet* magazine.

'How you feeling?'

'Oh, Tommy love, at last. Let's get gone before they bring that sandwich trolley.' She was obviously thinking straight, even though she was slurring a bit. 'Have you had anything?'

It went without saying that I hadn't. Trying to avoid her dressings, I helped her into her clothes and into the wheel-chair: she was so light, as if she was totally empty. She gave a little wave to everyone as I wheeled her out.

Driving home, I glanced across to see she was snooz-ing, her head thrown back, mouth open wide like a hungry chick, and I put the radio on quiet. I'd been the family driver since I turned seventeen, Dad presenting me with the keys to our old Sharan as if he couldn't wait to get in the back with Beth and the twins. It'd been the same with the bills and stuff. One parents' evening the school mentioned me maybe doing Maths AS-level early, and that weekend Dad handed over all his piles of paper and his notebook that he'd written PASSWORDS/PIN NUMBERS on, clapping me on the shoulder like I was finally becoming a man.

The kitchen was cold but felt freshly deserted, the tang of pickled onion Monster Munch staining the air. I knew it was hard for Beth to stop the twins: one would help the other onto the worktop to reach the cupboards, and I'd even come in once to find Kenny grilling cheese on toast, watching it through the glass with his oven gloves ready like a proper little expert. I didn't like leaving Beth in charge, especially as she benefited from me being around too – in terms of rules, keeping to them, and cupboards, keeping out of them.

I wheeled Mum through to the stairlift so she could go and have a lie down. Beth heard me put the kettle on and shouted from the telly room that she wanted two sugars.

Two matching notes on the table:

Dear Year 3 Parent or Guardian,

For our pre-Easter trip next month, we'll be taking the children to the wonderful world of Flamingo Land! We do hope you'll let your child participate, as we always find it stimulates a lot of excitement as well as beneficial classroom activities such as animal projects, colour work, introduction to simple physics concepts, etc. Only £27.50 per child. Please send full payment by the 20th at the latest.

The only thing to do was quickly hide these in the sideboard – otherwise the twins would start hoping, and I'd have another of those conversations to look forward to: Lily sniffing and wobbling, Kenny kicking the skirting board.

Dad's key turned in the door and he came in, that Dadly fondness in his thin face.

'Alright, Tom. What's that, then? Premium bonds come up, have they?'

'Yeah, right. Just school letters.'

'Your Mum alright?'

'Oh, you know.'

Dad nodded as if this was good. We'd been through four previous ops with Mum and although this one wasn't the worst, she was running out of things to have taken away. I'd never asked Dad if he might volunteer instead, but maybe that time was coming.

'Daddy!' Lily hurled herself across the kitchen towards him.

'Daddy, Daddy!' Kenny shouted, 'Flamingo Land!'

Oh shit.

'What about Flamingo Land?' he said, grabbing one in each arm and mashing their small faces against his chest.

'There's a school trip! Everyone in the whole world's going.'

'Well, isn't everyone in the whole world lucky?'

I turned to deal with the boiling kettle, got everyone's favourite mugs lined up.

'Kenny, Lily,' I said, calling them out from under Dad's armpits. 'What kind of twins are you again?'

They shrieked and piled over each other to get out and upstairs.

We had this thing: I'd say, or trick them into saying, *non-identical*, and they'd walk into it every time because they took it so seriously – who they were, how they came to be – and then I'd dive at them, fingers first, saying *what? What? Non-iden-TICKLE?!* I didn't even have to say the full thing any more. It killed me the way they squealed and squirmed.

Beth filled the doorway as they scrambled up the stairs. She was wearing those peach-coloured trousers that made me wince, and she tugged at her crotch when she saw my face.

'Mum texted to say she'll just have it black.' At Christmas we'd drawn lots to see who could have the phones, and the winners were Mum and Beth.

'Okay. Do you still want sugar?'

'Yes. Why?'

I stirred it in for her, handed over the two mugs. 'Let me know if she wants anything else.'

'Obvs.'

She sloped back into the telly room. We used to call it the living room, and we used to mute the telly when the adverts came on, and we'd eat together at the table – with Radio 4 on – but we kind of let all that go when Grandma finally died.

I put Dad's mug in front of where he sat. 'Don't get them all excited. It's nearly sixty quid.'

'Ach–' He has this habit of waving away complete impossibilities as if they're just bad smells.

'We can't...' I started.

'Tom, son, don't be so... We're going to have a good month this time. I can feel it. Look at me!'

He stood and pulled his shirt against his torso, sucking in air, and crabbed his arms like a bodybuilder. A curve of ribs, a hollow, the shock of his belt buckle.

'Dad.'

'I'm down a whole notch, you know. At work I have to sit on a cushion.' He winked. 'The future's bright, kiddo. Go on, do your sum thingies, just see what comes out. You can put me down for a straight sixty kilos. Yes! I reckon, don't you? Then with your Mum, I mean, the swelling and that'll be gone by Monday, she can't come out more than, what, forty-five now, can she? And then there's, there's–'

He trailed off when his thoughts reached the four of us. He dropped his voice. 'How's Beth?'

Beth – well. The old Beth was under there somewhere, the one I used to bounce with on the trampoline when we were small. She'd clutch my slightly bigger hands in hers and we'd jump and she'd giggle up into my face, so delighted, until I nearly wanted to die with happiness. But she wasn't small any more. And I hadn't heard that laugh of hers for months.

I tried really hard not to get on her case, but as she'd widened into her teens she'd really become a problem, Formula-wise. What made me mad was that she did it to herself, she kept doing it, and she hid it. I'd go in to join her watching telly and catch her stuffing something down the side of the settee; she'd crush Creme Egg foil into tiny nuggets before putting them in the bin. It was pointless – I still knew what they were – we all did, we were fine-tuned to those special confectionery colours, all of us on a hair-trigger of sweet wanting.

I admit I had my own bad habits: at work I'd pick the biggest jacket potato I could see, smush three pats of butter into it and, if the right canteen lady was on, get cheese as well as beans. So it's not like I didn't understand where Beth was coming from. But don't teenage boys need more food than, like, anyone? And I'm not being funny, but at least my clothes had a bit of leeway, unlike hers.

Basically, when it came to the Formula and all the hard work we did to get our numbers right each month, Beth kept messing things up. But it was all a nightmare, and right now I didn't want to get into it with Dad. 'Well, Assessment's this Monday,' I said, 'so I suppose we'll see.'

'We will that, son, we will that,' he said, happily.

I took my tea through to the telly room. The screen flaunted a close-up of a fork dividing a golden sponge pudding to release a melting centre, a velvety voice-over telling us how good it was. Beth stiffened. She was plopped low in the cushions, chewing the rope of her hair, one hank of thigh slumped over the other. These days that's all she did: just sat, texting, with this furious air about her, jagged lines daggering around her head. I checked her phone once when she went to the loo – I was worried she was getting into arguments at school, or being bullied on the social media she said she hated – but it turned out she was in about twenty different Whatsapp chats and her contributions were long and witty, full of quick, sharp comments and clever emojis. So it seemed the fury that hung around her was just for us.

Someone would have to say something soon, but no one wanted to tell her directly. I definitely didn't – she'd bite my head off. Dad would never shake himself into it, and Mum, well, Mum would rather have something else removed than make one of us feel bad. Still, if Dad was right and he was coming in under sixty kilos... maybe it wouldn't have to be this month, or next month. Maybe we could hold out until

April and the twins' birthday, which would put us in the next category and give us a tiny bit of breathing space before the shit hit the fan and we were put in Special Arrangements.

I heard the twins thudding around upstairs, giggling, and I had to scrunch my eyes shut at the thought of that.

The adverts finished and some programme called *Sick – or Trick?* came back on for its second half. Beth flicked her chin at the telly and said, 'Stupid idiots,' and I knew she didn't mean the poor bloke with stage 4 cancer, or the woman who was agoraphobic, who'd been told they were fit for work; she meant the white-toothed presenter and his handheld-camera team who were shouting through their letterboxes for comment, waving court papers in their grey, frightened faces.

Two nights after, Dad came in and shook my arm, whispering so he wouldn't wake the twins in their bunks. 'What's the number now, to ring for a doctor?'

His face was pale in the strip of light coming between the curtains. I knew it was Mum. I followed him to the bathroom where she was hunched in her wheelchair in her nightie, eyes squeezed shut, one hand twisted backwards to grip the edge of the sink. A thin, high sound was coming out of her and I had to swallow and look back out into the hall before I could go in.

I put my arm around the bones of her shoulders and told Dad the new out-of-hours medical advice number. He stood in the doorway and rang it on speakerphone, but there was a message saying the advice service had closed down, please phone your GP. I thought it had only been going a few months, but anyway, Dad did what they asked. The GP's surgery message gave us their opening hours and advised ringing the out-of-hours medical advice number.

'We must have got it wrong,' said Dad, and went to phone back, but I told him not to bother, and I sat holding the damp strands of Mum's hair as she leaned from her wheel-chair over the loo. I could feel the heat coming off her. She smelt like vinegar and off milk.

'I don't think this should be happening,' Dad said. 'I don't think this is right at all.'

Mum, panting, turned her head towards him and tried to say something, then retched again and groaned. With her new stitches every gip must have been like a knife stabbing.

She finished throwing up and sat shivering. Dad seemed stuck in the doorway. 'Can you get her a clean nightie?' I asked him. 'The one in the airing cupboard should be dry by now.'

'Oh! Yes, son, of course.'

While he shuffled around in the airing cupboard I stripped off her soaking nightie. Her eyes were rolling but they met mine for a second and I wanted to make a joke of it, something about me having to see her naked and her having to let me, anything to make it a bit better, but I couldn't say anything except something pathetic like it's okay. I was busy thinking Right, Tom, practical steps: get Mum comfortable, find out what's wrong, get the solution, get things back to normal. She whimpered as I lowered her naked body back down to the plastic of the wheelchair and I nearly lost it. Do not fucking lose it, Tom. I had to loosen her fingers – she was holding onto me like I was the edge of a cliff – so I could turn and get the shower running warm. Finally, Dad came back in, waving the clean nightie, and I got him to help me lift her onto her special shower seat and told him to help her get clean and dry. He could manage that.

I knew we hadn't used up all of February's internet credit, so I went down to the kitchen and dug out the Procedure Unit's scribbled discharge note to remind myself exactly what she'd had done this time. I Googled *problems post-hysterectomy*, *partial hepatectomy*, *cholecystectomy*. Antibiotics seemed like the first option. I'd pop down to Anwar's before work and get them; I had an old prescription I'd managed not to use.

If she was still like this in a couple of days, though, we wouldn't make it over to the FHO for Assessment on Monday. It wasn't technically the end of the world to miss an appointment – they'd let you miss one a year, enter your own provisional data online, and they'd sort it all out at the next appointment – but it meant I'd have to officially do the Formula myself.

Even unofficially doing the Formula gave me a headache. I did it each month between Assessments to see where we were; I'd get out the Family Guide and the calculator and plug in our info. It meant each month I had to chivvy the twins to get on the scales – the worst weight of three, I'd take – and get a written note from Beth, after asking about a million times, because she wouldn't tell me her number to my face. She only gave in because she knew Assessment would reveal everything anyway, and we'd had enough bad scenes in the past after a surprise result – all of us sniping blame, storming through the waiting area past other anxious, dehydrated families. We'd drive home in silence, staring out at the golden arches, the Wild Bean cafés, the ten-metre hoardings sighing *eat, eat* – but not stopping, because we didn't have the spare calories, and having just failed Assessment for the month, we wouldn't have the spare cash. No one wanted that kind of surprise.

The online timer told me I had a while still, so I went to the DWP website to check for Formula updates. They changed it every now and again, so you never knew: an early threshold change, maybe. But no. I logged in to college, to see how far behind I was. Then email, but no surprise pay rise announcement, ha ha, and no secret admirer messages from fit local girls, ha even more ha. Finally, I went to look at the news, because Mum never let us put it on the telly anymore. When she was with us downstairs she'd veto anything other than David Attenborough or Strictly, and we could hardly argue.

Dad appeared behind me as I skimmed the headlines.

'Oh dear,' he said. 'There's always someone worse off, eh?' And he gave my shoulder a squeeze.

I turned, so he'd stop.

'Well,' he said, 'your mum's settled down. Better get to sleep myself if I'm to be up and at 'em tomorrow, eh?'

Something flared up in me as he ambled out. His relentless happy-man good humour. He never seemed to stop and question his life: our tiny terrace, his embarrassing job in the recycling plant. He used to teach art history at the uni, but somehow got himself made redundant, and then something happened to his personality and it was like he couldn't get back to where he was before. Grandma used to call it 'a little local difficulty' and turn her nose up and change the subject.

I'd only ever heard Dad say there was a lot of competition out there, a man couldn't expect to be on top all his life, he was lucky to even have a job, blah blah. 'There's zero stress in this job, so I can focus on my book.' His book, as he called it, sat on the shelf above the sideboard in a lever arch file, sort of looming. I'd never seen him touch it, though I remember him a few years ago shut in the bedroom during the day, Mum saying he was trying to write. I suppose we were living on his redundancy then – I was only eleven, I didn't think about it – and then Mum got her little surprise, then the bigger surprise that there were two of them, and it all coincided with the Formula coming in, so he had to find something and the recycling plant was all there was at the time. Then he just settled for it. We struggled month after month and Dad just said, 'Ah well. No fault of our own.' Maybe not, but he never thought about whose fault it was, or if there was anything we could do about it.

I was starving. I went back to bed.

After dropping Beth and the twins at their schools, I headed to Anwar's. Although it was going on for nine, his shutters were down, which was worrying. We'd been using Drugworld for a while because it was next to the big Asda, but I'd stopped at Anwar's for paracetamol a few weeks ago and he was open then. I got a lucky parking space and sat looking at the dead shop. Anwar was never exactly joyful, especially since his family was made to go into Special Arrangements and his granddaughter got put with a family of vegans in Colne, but that day he looked really grim, told me Drugworld had put in some official query about his dispensing licence. Troublemakers, he'd said, bullshit merchants. It sounded funny in his accent, coming from under his kind white moustache.

I drove off to the retail park. Drugworld, so brightly lit,

had the biggest range of everything you can imagine. A relief: Mum would get what she needed today. The price of prescriptions now, though. After I paid I had to sit down for a minute on the plastic waiting chairs. I must have had my head in my hands, because I didn't see Erin until she was standing right in front of me saying my name in this concerned way.

'Oh,' I said, sitting up.

'Alright?'

'...Yeah.'

'I'm just getting...' She lifted her basket – four different flavours of Slimfast, which no way did she need.

'Right. I had to get some stuff for my Mum.'

'She have another op?'

'Yeah.'

She nodded.

'How's Beth?'

'Alright. You know.' I always sounded like an idiot when I talked to Erin, but she nodded again. We said nothing for a minute.

'So how's college? Top of the class?' she said, jaunting out one hip.

I got a little flip in my stomach. 'Ha, yeah. Well, actually not really.'

'Come on.'

'No, I haven't gone for ages, had extra shifts and that.'

'I bet you'll get all A-stars anyway, with your big maths brain. You love all that stuff, don't you?'

Some old woman with a crutch came up, aiming herself at my seat.

'Well, I'd better...'

'Yeah.'

'See you.'

Last June, I'd helped her revise for her exams, lying on the grass outside her flat. I was trying to find another way to explain binomials when her boyfriend turned up on his bike and I got up to go, but she told him she was going to be busy all day and after he'd gone she nudged me in the side and gave me this long look. It was the moment, but I'd not said anything, not done anything. Now, as I watched her walk off towards the self-checkouts, I kicked myself yet again.

Mum started to get better after a week or so, but we'd missed Assessment. So after work on the last day of February, instead of going to college, I sat at the kitchen table and did the Formula.

When the Formula first came in, I found Dad hunched over the Family Guide, close to tears. The Guide helps you make your own Action Plan to pass Assessment, and it includes the actual Formula they use. I'd sat down with him and had a look, tried to explain it. Each family member gets a number of points, depending how their weight compares against the national average, given on tables in the back of the Guide. You add them all together and you get a number, W, which you plug in to the Formula:

$$\frac{W}{(N+A)} * \left(1 - \frac{((N - 3*INT(\frac{1.1}{(1+2^{-N})}))}{N}\right) + 25 * (A - 2)$$

Where N is the number of children, A the number of adults and so on, obvious. There's a penalty for one-parent families, and, hard cheese for us, a penalty for having more than three children. Dad rang up to double-check about the twins, because he couldn't believe they really counted as two, but they did. To be fair, I could see the logic both ways.

If you achieve your ideal weights, you get your full amount, but if you fail it's cut, really cut. Then, if you keep on failing, Special Arrangements.

It was a bit complicated, the Formula, and that's what had upset Dad – not understanding the maths. Once he saw I could do it, he relaxed. But that was the problem. There were two horrible months in a row where we all seemed to have a growth spurt and we failed – took us a year after that to get straight with the payday loan people – and Dad didn't get that if we kept on the way we were going, they'd break us up. I wanted to hammer it home to him, but whenever I tried to talk about it he'd wave his hands in the air and do a stupid Halloween voice – 'Ooh, Special Arrangements!'

Now, sitting at the table with the calculator, I put my pen down and sat for a minute with my eyes closed. Even after everything Mum had done, even though I'd gone all day without any water to cut a couple of pounds, we weren't going to make it.

I'd have to go online to enter the final figures, but I couldn't bring myself to do it just then. I drank a huge glass of water, then refilled it and joined the others in the telly room. Jamie Oliver was on, beating a massive steak through some cling film with a rolling pin. When he'd finished, beaming, the ads came: stuffed crusts oozing mozzarella, buckets of crispy chicken. Then came one of those low-quality montage adverts, showing stills of local Easter attractions: the model railway, the mining museum, the petting zoo.

'So,' Dad said. 'Flamingo Land?'

'Dad!'

I couldn't believe him. A fortnight ago I'd had to say no
– Lily had cried for two hours – but they'd moved on, the
twins, and accepted it. Now they sat up and looked at each
other as if they'd heard Santa's sleighbells.

'Oh Tom,' he waved me away, 'let them tell me about it.'

Kenny panted down his mouthful of Five Alive. 'It's the
whole of Year Three, it's like a whole day and we have to go
in a coach at six o'clock in the morning!'

'It's half past six it sets off, Kenny,' Lily said. 'But Tom
said we can't go.'

'Well,' said Mum from the corner, looking at me. 'Let's
see. It's a whole day? Won't you need a packed lunch? And
a bit of spending money?'

Kenny was already shaking his head, his eyes wide.
'Nope, there's this place there where the children go, to eat,
they have crocodile soup and pelican pie and like, armadillo
something, I can't remember, but you get this like voucher
for the shop too, and Miss said to tell our mums and dads it
was all inclu– inclusied.'

Mum and Dad glanced at each other. The twins jumped
to the edge of their seats.

'Tommy?' said Dad, 'How's it looking?'

I drank some water, tried to steady myself. 'Well, I put all
the numbers in –'

'Did you put me in at sixty?'

'Yeah, sixty dead on, and Mum at forty-five –'

'Oh, I don't even know if I'm that, now,' Mum said, and
she went into this coughing fit. Beth got up and rubbed her
back for her.

'But, you know how complicated it is, and I mean, we're
all still growing, even me –'

I was trying so hard not to look at Beth.

'So,' Dad said, 'what did you come up with? We'll get our full lot this month, won't we?'

'I can't– I don't know exactly.'

Then Lily turned her small face up to me. 'Is it– So are we still not going?'

Seal pup eyes.

I filled in the online form, ticked the box to swear the numbers I'd entered were true and accurate, sat for a minute before I clicked submit, and then it was done. No alarms went off, no police came to the door.

It felt so nice, a week later, to log in to the account and see a positive figure. It felt completely new to have two purple twenties in my wallet, to actually plan for real how I was going to ask Erin if she fancied a drink sometime, maybe even a Pizza Express. And it felt amazing to be able to tell the twins they could go on their trip – we had a whole evening at the computer, the twins leaping all over my knees, poking their fingers on the screen and turning to me open-mouthed at the sights and promises of the theme park wonderland – and to send them off to school the next morning with a cheque each in their little backpacks.

And then somehow, like any month's money, it just ebbed away. Dad a bit freer with his debit card; Mum's internet bits and bobs she'd been waiting to get; cash for store cupboard stuff; petrol at Asda; shoes for Kenny and Lily; the standing orders; bit by bit it dwindled, and then it was all gone.

In the Family Health Office there was a big green poster headed *The Fantastic FORMULA for Family Fitness!* Clip-art party hats and streamers either side of the header, and a graph. I stood up to have a proper look. Before I realised why, I felt my face go red, there was this scent I recognised and I turned round, and it was Erin with her sisters and her Mum.

'Wow – hi.'

'Don't normally see you,' she said.

'They changed our day. Because of Mum, the other week?'

'How's she doing?'

'Better. Thanks. You going in?'

'Yep, when they call us.'

'What do you think?' I nodded toward the Assessment room.

'Oh yeah, we're well under. What about you? Did you have to do it yourself? What do they do today then, just confirm what you put in?'

'Yeah yeah, should be good, should be fine, it worked out okay, it– yeah.' Nodding and nodding, toeing the nylon carpet. It probably *would* be fine; we'd been so close to the line I'd only had to round down a tiny amount to get us under.

'Pain, innit? It does work, though.' She nodded toward the graph and its downslope. 'Says BMI rates have gone down so they're going to reset all the averages soon.'

It was like a silver bell in my brain. But there was another thing biting at me – now or never Tom, or you are an utter waste of space. 'Look, I wanted to ask you something, are you, would you –'

'Taylor-Peel?'

We were being called in. It was the Assessor with the ankles and the shiny hair down the back of her white coat, and I didn't want to keep her waiting.

Someone had left one of those tipping trolleys full of plastic crates on the wheelchair ramp, so me and Dad carried Mum down the steps. It was snowing again, settling on the slope of daffodils behind the rank of cars. Kenny and Lily bundled each other through the revolving door like they had when we'd come in, but quiet. With a jerk of my head I got them to follow us. Beth was already at the car, jabbing at her phone.

I wasn't going to be the first one to speak. Whatever I said, Beth would say I was having a go at her. And, well, I *would* be. It was her fault. She was the one who cost us so much in food, the one who'd done most to take us over the line today, the one who just kept getting heavier like she didn't care.

I slammed my door. As I reversed out of the car park, scattering slush, Dad muttered, 'Steady on, Tom.' We set off on the ring road, first drop-off the twins' school.

The fit Assessor had smiled nicely as she handed me the leaflet about Preparing for Special Arrangements. She also gave us an updated Family Guide. What Erin had said was true: thanks to the success of the Formula, average BMIs were down, so the points tables were going to be adjusted in a couple of months.

Erin was still in the waiting room as we left, and I wanted to stop and say, hang on, think about it, if they're going to make the average lower, wouldn't everyone who was doing just about okay suddenly be above average? And then be guaranteed to fail Assessment? But of course it couldn't work that way, surely, that would be stupid, and unfair. And anyway, I'd remembered Erin's mouth twisting up funny when she said about my big maths brain, so I hesitated. And then the Assessor had bent over to unbolt the double doors for Mum's chair and we'd had to thank her and go.

Of all people, it was Dad, sitting in the middle seat, who started. 'I s'pose we have to, then.'

I still didn't say anything. I was thinking about the Special Arrangements leaflet, how it would tell us whether we'd have any choice, or whether they chose for us, and if so, how; whether we could visit; how long it would go on for – all the terrible answers to all the terrible questions would be in there, but how would I even be able to look at it?

'Can we, Tom? Can we pay it back?'

'Not really, Dad, no.' Even if somehow we could avoid Special Arrangements in the future, there was the problem we'd come away with today, which was that we had to pay back the money we'd had last month, after I'd done the Formula.

'We kind of spent it, didn't we, on staying alive.'

Lily whispered something no one could hear.

'What'd you say, sweetheart?' said Dad.

'Are we not going to Flamingo Land now then?' Her little voice, full of hope and hopelessness at once.

I couldn't help it then. 'No. I'm sorry, but you'll have to go tomorrow and ask the school for the money back, because none of us can have anything nice now, can we? Not when we need that money so we can keep eating and eating, and pretending we're not, and pretending everything's fine.'

Beth in the far back seat pulled out her earbuds. 'Well, it's not *me* who pretends everything's fine. Don't blame *me*.'

'Course not, lovey,' Dad said. 'No one said it was your fault.'

'You don't have to say it though.' She was rattling the seats in front of her, almost standing. 'I can see the way you all look at me, like I'm the problem. Like you want me to die.'

Kenny's voice was high. 'Don't die!'

'Don't die, Beth!'

'Beth's not going to die, Lily, Kenny, it's all right.'

'But you all want me to. Admit it. It'd all work out if it wasn't for me and my big fat disgusting body.'

'Beth, please, sweetheart.'

'If anyone's going to die anytime soon, I think you'll find it'll be me.'

Mum's voice was so small these days, but it cut through us all. I turned so fast to look at her that I screwed the wheel round too far and nearly drove onto the pavement. I stamped the brake, and the sudden shock of the stop made Lily finally start crying.

I had thought it'd be all right. I had thought we'd match up today with what I'd put on the form – really, we'd been so close, it wasn't fraud. But they'd told us it wasn't all right. And now they were changing the rules, because they could do whatever the hell they wanted, as if the country were some fantasy land for them to play around in and we were all just cartoon characters.

'Beth, it's not you. It's never you,' I told her in the rear view mirror. And I meant it. Beth was so bright, so pretty, when you actually looked at her. It killed me that she had so many friends, attracted all that love for being who she was, while we all silently punished her for the same reason. Maybe she sat in the telly room and ate, but it wasn't laziness, I suddenly realised, it was an act of giant rebel energy. Refusing to play by their stupid rules, refusing to let them reduce her. Thank fuck one of us had some resistance in us.

We were more or less in a lay-by so I turned off the engine. 'It's my fault, I must have done the sums wrong. I don't know. The really big problem is, next month, and the month after – they're changing the rules, we'll be way over the average, I don't know how we can...' I stopped and took a breath. 'It's all right. There'll be some way... I'll sort it. I'll get another job. Dad, maybe if you, you could' – and a big lump came up like I was about to be sick, but I swallowed it and carried on – 'Dad, you've got to get a better job. You could earn so much more.'

'But Tom, I –'

'No. You've got to at least try. Look at Mum! And Mum, you've got to stop doing this. Those so-called Procedure Units... I'm not going to take you again. Look at the state of you...'

Mum got hold of my fist that was beating the dashboard. We sat like that for a minute. Kenny reached over the back of my seat and stroked my neck with a little finger. I glanced at him in the mirror. Lily had crawled onto Dad's knee and was sniffling into his chest. The windows started steaming up as traffic zoomed by.

I reached round, clawed my fingers. 'What kind of twins are you again?' And I got the instant sunlit squirm from them both.

Behind us all, Beth unsnapped her seatbelt and opened the door into the road.

Shit.

I scrambled out and dashed after her. Cars were honking all over the place. It was the ring road, for god's sake, slippy already from the new snow. She skipped the crash barrier and stopped as if to check the traffic but she looked down at herself, not at the road. A bus slowed right in front of me and I was faced with a giant Lindt ball being filled with molten caramel, blocking my path.

I got this sort of surge.

I saw exactly what the driver shouted as I ran round. I skidded to the barrier. Beth stepped out into the other roadway but I did it, I got her, I grabbed her arm, then I pulled her to me and just hugged her soft self. We were there a full minute, ten minutes, a lifetime, in the slackening snow, between the oblivious streams of cars. Eventually I felt the buzz of her speaking into my chest. I let her go. Her nose was running.

'Where you going, you big idiot?' I said.

A probationary little smile. '...Burger King?'

'—'

'Joking, duh.' She semi-punched me, wiped her nose with the underside of her wrist, and then the smile came properly.

I hugged her again. I glanced back at the car, at the pale faces of our family. Beth squeezed me with her strong arms, squeezed and squeezed until some life came back into me.

On Saturday as the streetlights blinked out we were all back in the car, sitting in the same seats but going the other way round the ring road, heading for the A1, everyone jigging about to Jessie J. And I thought about February's money that we'd have to give back and March's money that we wouldn't get, and then what was looking more and more likely, Special Arrangements, the twins, how would we, how could we? Unless that other party got in and stopped the Formula. I mean there were elections coming, my first time voting, so.

The evening of the failed Assessment, I'd hoovered in the telly room and moved all the furniture around and we'd had a family meeting. Mum sat propped on cushions in the big armchair with the twins on her lap, Beth and me sat together on the small sofa, and Dad brought in a kitchen chair but actually stood up as he tried to come up with some ideas about what we might do. We talked for a couple of hours, no rules, everyone got to say what they wanted to say.

In the end we all agreed. There was nothing we could do.

I was surprised at some of the things that came out of my mouth. Like the idea about this weekend – that was me.

'But Tommy love,' Mum said, with a little laugh, 'after everything, we can hardly afford that.'

'Technically, we can't afford to *eat*,' I said. 'So what do we do? What do they want from us?'

'*Yesss*, Tom,' Beth hissed then, digging her nails into my knee and shaking it.

Driving up there now, seeing the first sign which made the twins scream so hard that everyone laugh-shouted at them to shut up, I thought about how I'd put our petrol on the credit card again, and that we'd have to pay full admission price which was like eighty quid for a family, no schools discount, and then there'd be hot dogs and milkshakes and soft toys and branded pencils from the shop. I thought about how we'd have to sneak Mum onto the Octopus because there was a height minimum, and for a second I wondered whether we should just have let the twins go with school instead, and whether this whole thing wasn't a massively irresponsible, maybe even illegal, thing to do. And then I pictured Lily and Kenny screaming happy in the whirly teacups, and Dad reaching for Mum's hand in the café, and me and Beth the spitting image of each other in the gormless photo they take of you at the scariest bit of the Doomacoaster, and us all pointing out the flamingos as if they were a surprise – clue in the name and everything – and so I thought, you know what? I don't care, because no one, not even the people with the power, can force things to be exactly the way they want them to be – not always, maybe not ever.

ON DAY 21

Nineteen days of rain – unprecedented, they said – and I could hardly tell it was morning. E, my youngest, was screaming. She'd had me up for four hours the previous night, so I switched her off, laid her on the bed and gently closed the door, the silence a soft blanket around me.

C and D were sitting on the floor of the living room in a junk of bright items, lost together in their intricate exchange of small powers and pleasures. The rain had kept us in, sandwiched between the flats above and below, and the weather lay so low that the window showed only the canal, slate-grey, slopping onto the towpath. I sat and started folding a heap of clothes warm from the tumble dryer. The heap shrank and the folded pile grew. I was running out of these neat, methodical tasks, so I took my time.

D threw a rampaging dinosaur at C, but it missed him and bounced off the leg of the tea table on which rested my laptop.

The machine woke with a surprised whir. It had slept

through the night, and for the first time in two weeks I'd managed to leave it alone all morning. A pair of half-folded corduroys hung from my paused hands as the screen grew keen. It was rich with tiny stars and hearts and numbered dots and exclamation marks.

Notifications can't be ignored. Each one is like a bullet – I mean a bullet that would come out of a gun, not a bullet in a bulleted list, although these seem to be related in terms of urgency. You have to deal with them or they nag at you. You have to deal with them or they might smash through your body. My legs stood me up and I went over to sit at the laptop.

Some time passed. C and D started pulling at my jeans. Their pleasant babble soured to whining, and at that moment the wind spat a great hard gobful of rain at the window. A sharp breath went out of my nostrils and I reached down and switched them both off.

The switch was my secret. I'd told myself I wouldn't resort to it so much, especially with E, who was already small for her age, and such a lovely, milk-scented little thing – though so were the other two; don't get me wrong, they were the sun in my sky. But the minutes of my days were long and difficult, full of complexity and murk, and the switch was a way to get through. It was a way to sharpen the edges of life, to know where and who I was when things got fuzzy. It cleaned; it freshened. Although what helped me wasn't the switching off as such, it was the fact of the switch itself. I'd come to rely on it. And now, for the first time, I'd used the switch on all three children at once.

I stopped for a moment as the implications threatened to come clearly into my mind, but I shook them off before they could. I arranged C and D's little limbs so they wouldn't

cramp. Then I returned to the laptop. It was the laptop
that had shown me the possibility of this kind of ease. Its
machine world was either/or, yes or no, on or off, zero or
one. It was the antidote to uncertainty: that devious mould
that grew everywhere if I didn't keep on top of it.

Dark had deepened the silence in the room by the time
my bladder forced me up from the chair. My phone was
there in the bathroom, where I'd left it last time I'd needed
to come in here while staying connected to the machine
world. The phone offered a sort of letterboxed version of the
yes/no world of the laptop, both pleasingly contained and
frustratingly miniaturised. I picked it up before sitting, and
as I peed I checked its various messaging systems. There
was a text from B saying he'd be home early. My husband
was a departmental head – some technical department, I
wasn't sure which: he said his responsibilities 'spilled over'.
When they pushed him to exhaustion I'd tell him he should
have boundaries, but he'd say it wasn't that simple. I didn't
see why not. He worked for a company, his days a grid of
meetings and targets; all of their work was in the service
of crisp, black numbers. It seemed to me that it should be
wonderful. B would sigh and look at me, so I'd move things
along, make him a drink, rub the tough tops of his shoulders as he hunched over work. I had only ever switched him
off once.

Just as I checked the time, I heard the squeal of the security gate three floors down. I flushed, washed, and ran in
to switch on the two older children, and then lastly, in the
bedroom, E. Her little fingers curled and grasped, and her
lips plumped back up as the flow of subcutaneous activity
restarted. This was the best bit about using the switch: for

those first few minutes my children and I were together and fresh again, and there was a kind of crystalline peace. I picked E up and rocked her as she blinked and jerked a fist toward the sweet oval of her yawning mouth.

B turned his key in the door and I went to meet him, and that night everything was fine.

On day twenty the sky lifted to dove grey, and I drove us out to the big Asda, spinning arcs of water from the wheel-arches. As I parked, the rain hardened again. C thought his cagoule felt 'squishy' and refused to put it on, then refused to be put into it. When he started shouting my fingers reached, so easily now, for the switch. Nothing happened.

I flicked it up and down, up and down, but nothing. I took hold of his contorting face and turned it to me, looking for an answer from him, as if he had overcome the switch by the force of his own will. This sudden gesture took him aback and he did in fact stop crying. For a second we held each other's gaze, and I was struck by the absolute strange-ness of him, this person who had come from me, and it seemed he saw the same strangeness in me.

I lifted his sister, D, from the other side. I tried her switch. Again, nothing happened. She squirmed away from me and went to peer into the tiny convex mirror set within the wing mirror, enjoying her own distorted face. E was asleep in her car seat and I didn't want to trouble her.

I looked around the car park, hoping perhaps to see another person in the same situation. The car park was tidily kept, with good space for each unit of car to sit quietly to itself, sure of its locked doors. Racing cloud reflected without sound in the rain-beaded roofs, and for a moment

I was calmed, the noise of the children dimmed. But there was no one to help.

Who exactly was I looking for? Someone like me or someone unlike me?

There was no one like me, I thought. All of the people I encountered during my days seemed fine, sloshing backward and forward with the tides of each day like happy seaweed. I, however, was up there on the surface, clinging to a broken raft, gazing into tarry liquid that would one day take me down. And that was with the switch to turn to. Now, if that had stopped working, I couldn't see how I'd be able to navigate the days at all. The laptop and my phone did much to help, but they wouldn't act directly on the children, these merchants of chaos who were forever plying their trade.

I didn't know what to do, so we entered the blue-white cavern of the supermarket – me pushing the trolley with E on the plastic seat, C and D trotting close to my legs – and I began to perform the shopping. Parallel lines of goods and lights. Staff dressed in clean white mesh aprons as if they were butchers and bakers. I soon clocked that I was the shopper in whatever scene they were playing out and the role began to feel like a good fit. Once the trolley was convincingly half-full, I felt safe enough to take an interval and I lay down on the floor between the long chest freezers. C and D ran up the aisle and down the ones either side, figure-of-eighting around the gondolas, and I was held by the cold white tiles under me and the cold white striplights above, and the pattern of the children running.

Soon, three people stood over me: a young male security guard, and two women like me. One was tapping at her smartphone. I felt a pull toward the pretty box in her hand, the universal object that could join the hands of everyone worldwide, and which, like the knife of a fugu chef, cleaned and sliced life into something that might not kill us.

The security guard felt for my pulse, which seemed unnecessary, but his warm hand on my wrist was nice. I smiled up at him. Yes, I was fine, and yes, these were my children; they were also fine. With kindness in his eyes he asked me whether I thought I could get up. Of course, I said, and climbed to my feet, straightening my clothes. The other adults drifted off, disappointed.

At the checkout, as I packed, D reached up for the handle of the trolley and started rocking back and forth, which looked like it felt good. I wished there was a trolley I could stretch up for, but of course I was grown, far too grown, and as I put my card in to pay I felt myself looming over the checkout, some giant redwood whose trunk was mostly rotted through.

When I got home I went to the laptop while the children ran about in their coats. Eventually they went into the kitchen, I registered noise, and I glanced up from the laptop as they came out carrying bowls, slopping milk and bits of cereal. They would be fine.

Time passed, and B came home. The scene made him stop on the threshold.

After he had tidied up the worst, B went out with the three children and I heard him drive off.

There was a period of heavy quiet and then he came back, carrying E.

The next thing I knew, B was pulling me to my feet, and

in the bathroom he put a toothbrush in my hand with the toothpaste already on it.

Once I was in bed, he sat on top of the bedclothes and said C and D were spending the night at his mother's. I said I was tired. He told me to get some sleep, but I didn't want to go to sleep.

– But if you're tired.

– Not that kind of tired.

He sighed.

– Tell me what happened.

– I don't know.

I did know. Everything was broken because I'd overused the switch – not just by using it on all three of them at once, but by using it so often, for so long. It was the accumulation of time I'd spent detached, from all of the messy world, as if I'd been flying and flying and inadvertently strayed out of the influence of gravity, and now I didn't have the fuel to get myself back to Earth.

But to explain would have meant explaining about the switch, and I was worried that the switch might just be a metaphor, that I was simply a bad and neglectful person. It struck me that I might be losing my mind. B waited for me to say something and I waited for him to say something, but neither of us said anything and eventually he turned off the light.

I woke several times with that same feeling of losing my mind: a tangible sliding sensation in my skull, as if it were a shallow bowl filled with fluid, in a neverending process of being nudged off the edge of a table. My fingers began to ache, and I realised I was gripping the edge of the mattress.

I went to the living room, entered the machine world of the laptop.

It wasn't yet dawn when B came in, shut the lid so fast I had to snatch my fingers away, and turned without speaking. I didn't think; I lunged for his neck, my thumbs on the nape and my fingers around his throat, on his hard Adam's apple. He grabbed my wrist and pulled one hand away, but the other still groped the back of his neck for a switch. Sounds were coming from me, and a sour heat I could almost smell. I expected to be thrown, shoved backwards into the furniture, but instead he reached behind him and took hold of my hand, firmly and warmly, as if he were pulling me up from a cliff edge over which I'd slipped.

We stood for a moment, two bodies in the sudden silence.

– It's stopped raining, he said. Come on.

With E asleep in her car seat in the back, B drove us through the lightening streets and out of town, taking the twisting hill roads and turning onto the lane above the reservoir. He stopped by a gap in the stone wall from where we could look down. The water was as high as I'd ever seen it, a plane of rippled steel under the dawn sky. The engine ticked.

– It's ages since we've come out here, I said at last. There's been so much rain.

His silence hollowed my words.

I carried on.

– Remember we went up on Saddleworth, and we put the tent up behind that wall and we couldn't hear the road, and no one could see us from any direction?

– Yeah, he said after a moment. That freezing night in midsummer. You wouldn't let me make a fire.

– I know, I'm sorry. I just wanted to have the night, as it was.

That summer I was pregnant for the first time and my new state came with the sudden understanding that yes, everything in the universe *was* expanding. We lay there for hours, outside in the cold, and it stayed light, and still light, like the night would never come. Stones dug into my spine through our blanket and the chill got right to my marrow; we held hands and I watched it come dark, and then the night seemed it would never end. Such deep cold in mid-summer: all the rules had been changed. The stars swam above us and I could easily have slipped off the hard ground into the billowing heart of the rest of existence, and I knew death would feel the same. I had nothing to hold on to, no certainty, and I had never been happier.

In the back seat, E stirred and shifted, then settled. With my eyes down, I told B about the shallow bowl of fluid in my skull, about flying out of the reach of gravity, the rotting redwood, the cold white of the supermarket floor. I told him about the seaweed and the raft, about the terror that textured my days, and finally I told him about the switch. Then I flung open the car door and jumped out and vomited onto the grass.

I used to live okay without the switch. We lived okay without the laptop. Then Ben brought it home, a fresh silver box swaddled in white polystyrene, and showed me the many ways in which it would improve our lives, and it did, and I gradually came to forget the time before, and who we were then.

Ben closed his door softly and stood over me, and a wind brought the clean scent of the reservoir. I looked up at him.

– I want to go back, I said.

My husband gathered me in, held my head against his chest. He whispered something, touched my hair. I have always liked his body, his man's body with its solid thighs, its uncumbersome chest, above all its neat and predictable rhythms. But in all my fleeing from the soft, the unnameable, I had forgotten there could also be this tenderness in him, and what allowing it to touch me might mean. I shook.

Evie began to wail, in her way that I understood meant nothing was wrong except she was lonely and afraid and bewildered to find herself where she was, and we would go to her, Ben or me, or both of us, in a minute. For now, the way his embrace pulled my head against him sent the texture of her cries through the bars of his ribs, resonant with the harmonics of her and him and me, and I listened as the hardly bearable music played out through that delicate instrument.

THIS PARADISE

They're good kids, but each time they fire that gun it seems they might be growing into something else. Or maybe she's just tired and her cramps are bad, making her see the worst. After all, Ollie and Sam are not her children; it's not her place to guess the way their genes might unfurl.

Between gunshots there's near-silence, just the waves shushing onto shore, the odd gull out by the reef. Hot air stirs the spindly pines. Cross-legged on the sand in the casuarina shade, Cara knocks a fire ant off her leg. The sun's a grill today: there's no cloud, no sign, yet, of the forecast tropical storm.

Ollie jumps every time Sam shoots, but he reaches out for the weapon afterwards. His arm seems no thicker than the barrel. He's eleven and likes drawing and keeps a tank of stick insects next to his bed. Sam shows him how to pump the air in, sight the centre of the beercan, hold steady, and take his time over the long pull of the trigger. Ollie has another go, but the pellet scuffs sand again.

None of them has been in a tropical storm before. In the eighteen months since they came over, the Atlantic's been unusually calm, as if nature can only focus on one disaster at a time, and although Cara works seven days a week, life on this lush island has been gentle, benign. When John and Geraldine sat her down this morning to talk about preparations they seemed mildly amused, the way people can be when their lives have never been under real threat – and Cara had to admit there was a thrill in it. People who'd been through it said it was terrifying, but what did that mean, really? Wouldn't there be something transcendent in it? Wouldn't it touch on the sublime, the sensual, being helplessly subject to some ultimate amoral force, with nothing you could do except let it come, full-on and savage? Perhaps natural destruction could hold a kind of beauty.

A dragonfly jerks to a stop mid-air and eyes her, then jets off. Sam starts sighting new targets – a coconut thirty feet up, a garbage bag just begging for someone to spill its colourful guts – but Ollie won't aim at anything but the can.

Bit by bit, they are learning wildness, exploring the relative freedom of island life. Geraldine often says how good all this is for them – so much better, she says, than that stifling health-and-safety-obsessed country we left. It's funny the way she calls it 'that country'. Perhaps naming it would bring it too close. It might risk ruining what they've managed to achieve by coming here: their escape no longer such a complete one, if the name of that country were allowed to hang in the air like an unbreathable mist.

The air gun was their father's. John's advice, handing it over, was *don't shoot anything anyone'll sue you for*. Inevitably, it's become Cara's job to put it away, and she always shakes a bit, particularly because no one's shown her how to unload the thing.

She checks her watch and calls, 'Five more minutes.' Geraldine's at home – her Saturday morning fundraiser's been cancelled for the school to turn itself into a storm shelter – and she'll notice if they're late back. Geraldine drives much of the charity work here; she mentioned her extensive charity interests in the original Nannies4U advert, as well as describing herself as a third-generation PhD (Cara's got used to her calling herself Dr E). She means well, treats Cara with an offhand kind of familiarity, though she can get pre-emptively defensive about certain things. More than once, unprompted by Cara, she's listed the reasons why she couldn't allow herself a career break, to have the kids, until she was forty.

'*No!*' Ollie grabs his brother's arm: Sam's aiming at a turkey vulture wheeling overhead. He shakes him off, but lowers the gun. He hands it over, and Ollie pumps it, aims again at the beercan, holds, fires. Misses. He shakes his head.

She's had worse bosses. The Ellands are relatively relaxed, and John's not over-involved. In Cara's experience, an involved father sets off about a million red flags and alarms. She dresses down and almost never wears make-up, but the way she looks – i.e. fairly symmetrical features, fresh skin, clear eyes, i.e. quite simply younger than the mother – has been known to cause ructions in other households. Here, though, John's happy to let Geraldine deal with her. He's an affable man, suiting his semi-retired late fifties, dealing with his investments each morning and snoozing each afternoon – which he uses as a joke: 'I used to be in the energy business, but not any more!' Geraldine guards John's office against the children but otherwise leaves him to it.

Down in the clearing, Ollie – white-skinned, vegetarian Ollie – gets a pellet in the heart of his beercan enemy and cheers.

She has half an hour before the boys' lunch. In the cool of her room she wakes the laptop and checks the news from home. They're saying that the proposed class action against WarmUtil could end up in the billions. This is good news, surely – she did sign that online petition – but then, if WarmUtil are proven responsible... She's tidied John's office when no one's there, did a particularly thorough job one time and was stopped in her tracks by the size of his shareholding. Of course, Cara is impeccably discreet, but, she thought in that pause, there's no rule against educating yourself. No rule against finding out what's being done in the children's names.

She found herself sitting in his plump leather chair and reading on, skimming the annual reports about well completion and potential new deposits, and trying to make sense of the dividend statements, their columns headed with comma'd strings of zeros to quietly indicate the true size of the small numbers beneath. WarmUtil have been generous with former board members like John. The Ellands, and those they can employ, are very lucky.

Cara knows this all too well. She's not just lucky to live here, but lucky to have been able to escape. If WarmUtil are brought down by this class action, who knows what would happen to their income, and then, to her. So she's been following the lawsuit story with her fingers crossed both ways.

Anyway, even if it did go ahead, the lawsuit wouldn't help

the people suffering now. And since reading John's paper-work and piecing together the impacts of his working life, the executive decisions he was part of, she's developed a need to read about that suffering in detail – as if by keeping informed she can claim, at some imagined future trial, to have been on the right side all along.

She does her usual search, scans the new results. Another cluster of lymphomas on the Wirral; one in Cornwall. Water queues erupting into violence. Regional hospitals reporting a big drop in the birth rate. Other reports – illustrated – of mysterious, aggressive diseases of the skin and soft tissues. And, as always, officials impugning the validity of all claims. She thinks of Mum and Dad, back in *that country*. They always put a good spin on things when they get through on the phone. Would it be that bad to go back? She thinks of Rob, but she's heard nothing since their awful lunch. She hopes he's found someone else; maybe there'll be a chance for him with someone else. Though they never got a defini-tive answer, she knows it was her body that was at fault.

The sun slants in. Cara goes out onto the small balcony. Jean-Chrétien is down in the garden, on his haunches, clipping the hibiscus planted round the base of the new pal-metto. 'Hi,' she calls.

The gardener looks up, then stands and waves. 'Good day, Ma'am.' The smile, like a crescent moon. The *Ma'am* takes her aback every time.

He stays standing.

'Hot day,' she manages.

'Yes, yes.'

'Garden looks lovely.'

'Yes, yes.'

'You work hard out here.'

He just does not stop smiling. What does it mean, this unchanging face he shows? She knows nothing about him, only that he's Haitian and he lives in a tiny lean-to which she saw once when she walked north from the house, off the track toward the cliffs. This wild, north end of the island seemed uninhabited when the Ellands bought their land, but it turned out a handful of Haitian refugees lived around and about – quite recent arrivals, most of whom would move closer to Williamstown as they settled, though the locals did not welcome them, and they lived in a kind of double exile. At some point John and Geraldine took on this surprise neighbour as an employee and Jean-Chrétien and his wife have stayed at the north end, with their square of vegetables, their two-room home of galvanize panels. The best that can be said about their house is that it has an uninterrupted sea view, but then, such views are not hard to come by in this paradise.

A hummingbird burrs across the balcony.

'Well.' She can't say 'enjoy the rest of the day' because he would be out here, working, under the blows of the sun. Then she recalls something. 'How is your wife?' She curves a hand over her abdomen.

'Oh, very good, very good. Thank you.'

'How much longer to go?'

'Thank you, yes.'

'The baby? How long?'

'Yes, yes. Good.'

After a minute she feels the sun start to bite beneath the skin of her arm.

'I think I'll –' She gestures.

He waves, bends back to the hibiscus.

She turns to go in, but sees the side door open. Ollie comes out and gives Jean-Chrétien a shy smile. He stands by the barrow and watches him work, touching the long handle of the loppers, full of silent expectation. The gardener stands and places his hat on the boy's head. He says something and Cara wonders how Ollie will understand him, but the boy replies enthusiastically and they carry on, chatting almost, as Ollie takes the pruning shears and follows Jean-Chrétien's directions.

As her eyes adjust to the dim indoors she sees she has left the laptop showing images of tumours, black and raw, violating body parts she can't identify, and she hurries to click out of the tab. Maybe she can't have what some other people have, but at least she hasn't got what some other people have got.

And sometimes she has to think of it that simply, because there's nothing more to be done. She's already looked for the Satan at the heart of it all. She's looked at all the company boards, the Cabinet at the time the extraction contracts were awarded, how their relatives and friends and contacts intersect. Yet all she can find, really, are human beings under pressure: from shareholders, from voters. These groups were human beings too: all worried about money, to a greater or lesser degree of desperation. Voters were householders, after all, sick of weighing up energy bills against kids' shoes. And huge numbers of shareholders were ordinary folk who'd bought into the not-to-be-missed government-subsidised share issue, after the briefly nationalised wells got re-privatised. Her own parents included.

She quickly checks the weather. Tropical Storm Michaela

has graduated. Extrapolations show *Hurricane* Michaela heading directly for their island chain, chewing it up tail-first, then taking a turn to the north-east, pushed by the jet stream away from the great, hot, American landmass. But the forecasters are getting excited: there's a chance she won't turn, and then Michaela will lick a great destroying tongue over Florida, Georgia, the Carolinas, then, if she has the taste for it, up the Eastern seaboard to New York, where all the damage that really matters will take place. Haiti has been struck horribly already, but then Haiti always is.

The house is certified to Miami-Dade hurricane standards, the corners of the windows stamped *Large Missile*, protecting against things that should never fly: coconuts; dustbins; those serrated stems of palm, so benign up there waving gently off the trunk, becoming weighty, ominous blades when separated from the mother tree. Even from a solid house, though, it's looking bad. It's maybe not as exciting as it was. It's maybe time to start thinking *oh no* instead of *ooh yes*. But all they can do is prepare, which basically means nailing down everything that isn't already nailed down and getting the hell out of the way.

She makes a list of jobs for the morning. There are things you can affect and things you can't; at 29, she's getting to know this.

Torrential rain on her windows throws her out of sleep, but she wakes into silence. Then the noise starts up again, for real: the percussion of PlayBox buttons under the battering thumbs of the boys. It's 1:45am. There are limits on their gaming hours and this is how they get around them. They wear headphones, of course, otherwise the house would resound with grenades and rocket launchers, the shrieks of dying enemies, but the boys can't help the odd yelp of joy at a particularly sweet kill, a moan of vexation at their own too-early deaths.

Permakult III is their favourite. The boys showed her you can fight in the regular army, deployed to defend a nuclear-power construction site, or in the Permas – guerrilla fighters whose vegan MREs and hemp uniform disguise the splatter-ing potential of their weapons. She'd sat alongside Ollie and they'd blasted the building site to bits, and though on some level she was shocked at the sheer range of killing options – was all that detail necessary? – they were, each one, unde-niable fun.

There's a muted *oh, ffff–* through the wall: Sam is dead. Pulling on her dressing gown, she goes and knocks softly on his door. As she pushes it open the boys look up in sync, fear whipping across their faces until they realise it's her.

'Sorry!' they whisper.

She shakes her head, failing to withhold a smile. Ollie scrambles out of his headphones as if Cara might still be fooled. She takes the controller from him and strokes his hair.

'Nearly two in the morning, lads.'

'Sunday tomorrow...'

'Nice try. There's loads to do in the morning, remember? You've got to help me with the shutters.'

She sees Ollie back to his own room. His eyes are bright. 'I got seven paras with one grenade, right, and it was amaz-ing, it made this massive hole in the fence and a load of other Permas came and ran in, and I got like this medal thing I've never seen before? And then all these helicopters flew over and started strafing us but I was weaving in and out –'

'Ollie!'

'What? Highest score ever, by miles.'

'All right, that's great, but it's bedtime now.'

He climbs under the duvet. Soon he'll be too tall for this bed.

'Can I show you something?'

From under the bed he brings out a big book – actually one of the old encyclopedias with which the interior decorator had lined John's office. Inside is a large folded sheet of artist's paper. He spreads it open over the duvet.

It's an extraordinary drawing. Actually, a collage – there are crushed petals, and what could be stamens sticking up from the page, along with some very accomplished impressions of faces she knows: Sam, their parents, Jean-Chrétien. (How quickly her eye scans for hers.) The faces frame a dark centre featuring uniformed characters from his games and a gas-masked crowd traipsing out from a ruined city.

'Wow, Olls. What is this?'

'Nothing. Just a thing.'

'I bet your Mum and Dad would be impressed.'

He looks up sharply, folds the paper and stashes the encyclopaedia back under the bed.

'Okay. You don't have to show anyone. Want me to tuck you in?'

'Okay.'

His hair is so fine and soft, she almost can't feel it under her hand. Sometimes, for a second, she has a glimpse of another life she's living, back home, where she and Rob are choosing pushchairs in John Lewis, spending the short winter Sunday afternoons feeding ducks in the clean frosted air of the park. Then she remembers where she is really, and why. Where her salary comes from. Flits of thoughts – there then gone – fine and soft and barely feelable.

They watched CNN together last night. The ongoing sexting senator story had made way for a new school shooting, details as horribly familiar as ever, except the perpetrator was just nine years old. The SWAT team had got him and he was in custody, apparently asking for his bear. Then, afterwards, the Atlantic weather, the whirling doughnut of satellite cloud, which put Geraldine into a kind of heightened state. When Cara comes in to do breakfast she's already up, sitting on the kitchen counter cross-legged in her yoga pants, swiping like a maniac through the iPad papers.

'We'd better go shopping,' she says.

Geraldine has never been inside Russell's, the island's one general store. The supply ferry comes on Wednesdays, so Cara does the main shop early on Thursday mornings. As the week goes by, Geraldine writes her an increasingly asterisked and capitalised list, then sits down with her to make sure she understands it, and Cara has learnt how to respond politely.

Having her in the passenger seat is weird, and Cara's eye keeps noticing her in the way fingers will keep roving to a lump growing where it shouldn't. She normally enjoys the weekly ride, breezing down the long scrub-lined road that spines the island, pretending the Jeep's her own. Half an hour of private air-con comfort and Coral FM. The scenery is relentlessly gorgeous but, if she's honest, much of the pleasure is in the profligate use of petrol, practically unobtainable back home by the time they left. Being able to fill up whenever she likes – no forms, no coupons, no hair-trigger queues – is one of the upsides of being here.

The land flattens out ahead of them. The eastern sky shrugs. Another day's coming. At the moment everything is calm and lavender-coloured, cloudfluff puffing sleepily over the nursery world.

Geraldine turns up the radio for the news, jiggling her knees. Michaela, now a Cat 3, has made landfall on the southernmost islands. So far there's little news of damage – yes, power and phone lines are down, but that's not necessarily a terrible sign. Utilities are already precarious on the outest of the out-islands. They're probably mostly okay.

Above them, nothing has altered in the innocent sky.

Ten minutes later they reach Williamstown, a designless collection of one-storey buildings, tilted road signs and low-slung power lines. When she first arrived at the international airport (international because of its two flights a week to Fort Lauderdale, Florida), wobbling down a pair of fold-out steps onto the tarmac and making her way to the peeling pink shed that was the terminal, she quickly had to scrunch up her expectations of what they'd been calling the 'capital'. But then, passport control took two minutes and her bags were waiting, so.

Outside Russell's a short queue has already formed. White retirees with ironed shorts and folded arms, a few native islanders in long sleeves and trousers, bantering with the store employees as they arrive for work. She parks under a streetlight, which happens to click off as they climb out. The warmth of day is pushing out the cool night. Can she feel something else on the breeze, a stirring, an urgency? Maybe.

Geraldine pauses on the threshold. The shelves were

already looking bare when Cara popped in on Friday, tired staff scooping cans of pigeon peas into a single row. Now the scraps of broccoli are yellow, all the fresh milk gone, just the powdered stuff left. Cara throws a couple of packs of spaghetti into the trolley with the 2-gallon water containers, rice, tins of tuna, grits. (There are always grits.) She has Geraldine's list, even though she's there with her. *Sugar, plastic wrap, bin liners, AA batteries if you can find, thanks, Dr E*. Dr E keeps disappearing down the next aisle and reappearing, like an anxious dog.

They join the queue for the till. A woman comes in with a newborn strapped to her chest. Cara waits for the inevitable: Geraldine patting her shoulder blade, giving her the sad smile.

'Mind you,' Geraldine says as if they're in the middle of a conversation, 'Sam and Ollie were a nightmare at that age. I really just missed being pregnant, you know? Suddenly they were out, crying all the time. Though it ruined my figure... I know it's a cliché, but. You wouldn't want to lose that, Cara. Luckily for me I've always been more about the mind.'

An elderly islander in front of them, hair chopped rough, clutches a basket with a pack of gummy bears, a tub of sour cream – where has she found that? – two wrinkled guavas, and five bottles of Chi-lay's Hot BBQ sauce. Cara imagines herself with the same basket, pictures the evening meal it would make. Stepping into another life again, just for a minute.

The man being served fumbles with coins. The till girl helps him count them out.

'Is it always like this?' huffs Geraldine.

'It can be quite busy at the weekend, yeah.'

She thinks of Saturdays when Mum used to take her shopping, holding clothes up to her on their hangers, treating her to a bun at the Debenhams café. Dad at home watching the final scores, kindly pretending to share her excitement in the small new things. These thoughts are meant to flit through, but as she stands here with her restless boss, a hint of off milk in the warm air coming off the refrigerator units and something sticky under her trainer sole, they stay, sharp, and a heat comes to her throat.

Suddenly, without thinking it through, she opens her mouth: 'Geraldine. Can I go home?'

'What?' Geraldine's foot-tapping pauses.

'I was wondering, maybe, might we plan for me to have a trip home? Just something short, to see my folks. It's been a while.' She bites her lip.

'Oh. Oh, Cara, really? It's rather dangerous.'

'They've moved, they're not in a bad area. Not as bad as some.'

'I don't know. I don't think it's wise. I'll speak to John, but don't go getting your hopes up.'

'...Okay. Thanks.'

Geraldine cranes to watch the next customer rub a thumb at the stubborn opening of a carrier bag.

'Really, though, we need to focus on the here and now. We're in a crisis, Cara. We have to remember that the boys come first.'

'Of course.'

'It's no time for being sentimental.'

'No.'

'So I don't really think it's something we should be

considering. Not just now.'

'No. Okay.'

Up at the house, she stows the supplies in the utility room.
The sense of the coming storm is more apparent here. Ooh,
the coming storm, ooh the emotional drama, but it really is
the weather she can feel, up on the island's exposed north
side. The Ellands' house is partly two-storeyed; its elegantly
doubled middle section watches over its ranging wings, and
at the very top is a weathervane shaped like a sailfish, which
is now wagging, looking disorientated. It's still what you
might call a beautiful day – when is it not, here? – but there's
something, a coolness, a just-perceptible dimming in the
pinks and reds and oranges of the bougainvillea.

The house sits in a kind of self-possessed quiet, con-
tented with its six bedrooms, its security cameras feeding
a panel of screens by the back door. No need for the razor
wire of the last house, the one the Ellands took a loss on so
their leaving wouldn't be delayed. The first time she saw this
place she was stunned, realising this would be her home
now, and that surge of glamour, knotted together with the
relief of having escaped, has never quite gone away.

But she didn't mean to end up here. She was supposed
to be a journalist – had trained for it – but she and Rob
graduated into the jobless aftermath of the second crash.
She spent a year as a kind-of-nanny for her cousin's friends,
which then slipped into more formal positions, which was
fine; it helped put food on the table. She and Rob were
happy and they thought, seeing as things were as they were,
they might as well have a couple of kids, think about her
career seriously afterwards. But during the horrid years

of tests and worry and living with daily pelvic cramps that never got fully explained, the profession she trained for pretty much disappeared.

Before the Ellands decided to move, before the awful lunch with Rob, she hadn't really thought about home and what it meant. That she lives on this gentle island is so fortunate – she loves the sight of every libidinous flower, every drowsy bee – but there are days when it's just a hot, muted backwater. Sometimes she'd like to feel drizzle, she'd like to smell a November bonfire, wake up to a frost. She is so ungrateful for her luck.

Cara holds the bottom of the ladder, agitated: she can't quite see. Sam's doing some semi-competent hammering but he keeps tutting, and a couple of dropped nails have plummeted toward her upturned face. Good to get the boys involved, though. In spite of the coming rain, Ollie's watering the parts of the flowerbeds the sprinklers don't reach, saying it's too sad when they droop. Geraldine has popped out to check their progress and is leaning against the wall of the house, in the shade, offering advice.

The sun roasts the back of Cara's neck. They keep the radio on; it's mostly music and Christian phone-ins, callers with respectless teenage sons and problem neighbours that Jesus blithely urges them to love, but every now and again there's a storm update. What news gets through from the out-islands is breathless, informal. 'The road is gone, the town is all gone, but we are alive, praise the Lord.' It reminds her of the first major tremors back home, and of when the leaked chemicals were, at last, acknowledged by the authorities. Days when newsreaders had faltered over their scripts, the media chaotic with disbelief at the extent of it.

Footsteps crunch down the drive. Geraldine and Cara
frown at each other. Then Jean-Chrétien appears. He's not
alone: his wife follows him, front-heavy and holding the hand
of a very small child who looks up at the house with huge
eyes. When he turns, Cara meets his gaze and smiles. The
glimpse of a smile comes back before he twists to hide in his
mother's long skirt.

She knows already why Jean-Chrétien is here, why he has
brought his family. She can see from Geraldine's jaw that
she knows, too.

'Jean-Chrétien, it's always nice to see you,' says Geraldine,
'but it's your day off.'

'Yes, yes.' He takes off his hat.

He looks up at Sam, coming down the ladder, and waits.

'Oh!' says Geraldine. 'Oh, I see. I'd better get Mr Elland to
come and speak to you.' Not for the first time, Cara wonders
why the many languages Dr E claims to speak don't include
French.

'Thank you, Ma'am.'

Hearing Jean-Chrétien, Ollie emerges from the flowerbeds. He nods shyly at the woman, then squats and shows the
little boy a heart-shaped stone he's found.

John comes out without Geraldine. He walks the gardener
a little way down the path, away from the watching eyes. John
talks. Jean-Chrétien listens. He waves his hat at the squat
little concrete block at the end of the garden. The shed has a
new, sloping roof, two slot windows under the eaves, an out-
door tap connected to the borehole. No toilet, but there are
buckets, Cara knows; it would not be impossible for a family
of three – three and a half – to spend a few hours there. But

of course, the Ellands won't hear of that – there are two spare en-suite bedrooms in their home.

John rolls his head as if working out a stiff neck, and then puts a friendly hand on Jean-Chrétien's shoulder and takes him back down the drive. Mrs Jean-Chrétien (how else is Cara to think of her?) grabs her son's hand and follows, without acknowledging Ollie's goodbye.

Ollie and Sam look at each other, look at the space where their father spoke to Jean-Chrétien. In a few minutes John's telephone undertones float again from the open office window. A bank of grey has appeared in the southern sky; a breeze is picking up, bringing the scent of the jasmine which tangles through their garden fence.

Ollie runs inside.

Cara hears his mother: 'This house isn't a homeless shelter, Oliver.'

'But he's not homeless, he just hasn't got a very good house. And he's my friend.'

'You'll understand when you're older.'

Sam is kicking the wall of the shed.

Cara starts to tell herself she's misunderstood what's just happened – that she must be wrong to imagine John and Geraldine would send the small family back to their galvanize lean-to. It makes no sense, when Geraldine had pointed to Cara's safety as the reason she couldn't go home – but her internal voice falters. It does make sense, actually; it's just one more refusal to consider a different course, by people who like to keep the reins in their own hands. Her jaw aches, but she knows she won't go in and say what she wants to say.

She tidies away the ladder, checks the storm prep list. They're mostly there. Sam's battening work is done, and the supplies are in. The skies are filling with active promise.

Twenty minutes later, as she's stuffing loose plant pots into a garbage bag by the shed, Cara hears from indoors both boys negotiating something briefly with Geraldine. Then the boys appear, with shoes and daysacks, and the air rifle in its case. There is a wildness in their tense fingers, even in their hair. They tell her they're going out, and she looks toward the house and frowns.

'Mum said okay,' says Ollie quickly.

Cara says, noticing for the first time that she has to look up at Sam, 'Well, all right, but you must be back in one hour. No more, do you hear me?' and she fills the request so full of love that she sees surprise in Sam's eyes as he hesitates, then agrees. She watches them push through the gate with an air of mission, clear and equal comrades in spite of their different heights. It strikes her for the first time that neither one really looks like their parents, which sparks an odd sensation, two parts satisfaction and one part foreboding.

She goes inside to Geraldine. 'Did the boys say where they're going?' she asks, as lightly as she can.

Geraldine is on her laptop, reading the latest report on the hurricane. 'Oh, they just want a taste of adventure, a bit of storm-chasing,' she says. 'They'll be back as soon as it starts raining.'

'I don't know,' says Cara. 'Shouldn't we –'

'They're big boys. Says here it's slowed down, and gone down to a Category 2, now. Because it's hit land. Might only be a 1 by the time it gets to us.'

That can't be disappointment in Geraldine's voice, can it?

An hour passes quickly while Cara finishes duct-taping

the vents. Two hours pass, and the skies are quite dark, and three hours pass, and the boys have not come back.

When Michaela gets to them in the early evening she looks like any other storm. Cara stands on tiptoe in the dry shower tray, opens the four-inch high window they didn't bother to shutter, peers out at the moderately blustery rain and allows herself a mote of relief. She's texted and called Sam's phone many times, but the signal's patchy already. Still, in this, they shouldn't be in too much trouble.

Then, as night falls, Michaela gets down to work. Cara's forced to close that little bathroom window, the four inches of connection to the outside world that were helping her stay hopeful.

It's the noise that's unbelievable. Cara had expected thunder, the thrill of lightning, but there isn't any. Instead this insistent, human-hating roar that just. Does. Not. Stop.

She is in bed, not with any hope of sleep, but she'd been sitting with Geraldine and John in the living room until she realised that the reason they weren't saying anything was not the drowning-out noise or the hurricane fear, but because they were waiting for her to go away. There were only so many times she could repeat how worried she was, only so many times they could counter with unlikely explanations for where the boys might be, safe and warm and forgetful, until they ran into silence. Their faces told her they didn't believe their own reassurances, and it made no sense that they should withhold their own worry from her – hold her apart, when they were all suffering the same thing – but for some reason they didn't seem able to give her that.

The wind is ludicrous. She clamps the pillow over her ears and tries not to picture them out there in the dark, trees rearing around them like snakes; please, let them have found shelter somewhere, anywhere. She thinks of Jean-Chrétien and his family and, a little late, includes them in her plea.

Her high-cornered room seems very square, holding a strange, empty stillness against the rage outside, like a cool cell at the centre of hell. The house is secure, the house is safe, the house is secure, the house is safe, but she feels more and more like an unearthed worm. She pictures the conchs at the kiosk behind Russell's, pulled live from their shells and chopped up with machetes. She wants to see how heavy the rain is – because there must still be rain, though she can't hear any. Just the wind, the wind, the wind, which has now gone beyond wind, turned into something that could come from a dragon. But she knows to stay away from windows, Miami-Dade standard or not.

The noise turns to screaming. The roof is trying to leave, tugged under the gutters by a monstrous hand. This is a Category 2? Even a 1? The human labels are laughably flimsy.

They should have stayed together and gone down to town, to the school, where of course Jean-Chrétien and his family must be, if they've found a way to get there. Surely a neighbour would have given them a lift, thinks Cara – then reminds herself it's they, the Ellands, who are their neighbours. They could have walked, she reasons, then reminds herself it's nearly twenty miles.

She should have stopped the boys going.

Cara's bedside light goes out with a *woof*. They've been on the generator since before the storm even hit, and either it's

out of oil or it's been ripped from its moorings or the side of
the house has fallen on it or the side of the world has fallen
on it. The unbelievable noise is amplified by an unbelievable
dark. Now she truly fears for herself as well as the boys.

England had seen atrocious weather in the years before
Cara left, but nothing like *this*. She'd always been able to
call the weird seasons an aberration, just as she's always
been able to forgive people, to ignore what they've done, but
this kind of thing changes you: you can't deny what's really
happening here, now, with the roof about to be ripped off.
Back in England, there was always the consoling thought of
emigration. Yet if land the world over is being chewed up by
the sea, and mild, verdant England has become a tremoring
sewer, and now absolute fury can come to this paradise,
then where is there left for anyone to go?

For a few minutes there's been a hammering, too regular to be part of the storm. Geraldine, John, knocking on
her door to check she's okay? No – that mad rattling is an
aluminium shutter, at the back, rocked again and again by
some desperate fist. She leaps in the dark towards her idea
of the door. Miraculously, her hand goes straight to the knob
and she's out, and in the cream-painted corridor she can see
well enough to dash down the stairs.

The living room is lit with torches. 'Stop,' calls Geraldine
– for Cara's safety, she assumes, then she realises that
something else is going on, something they don't want
interrupted.

John is standing near the back door, by the small screen
that shows the camera feed. All Cara can discern is an oval
shape, but she knows Sam's face. He and his brother are
huddled in the back porch; their father is talking to them

through the intercom.

John isn't moving. He isn't wrenching open the door and pulling his sons, these little pieces of the earth he lives on, into his arms. Cara unfreezes and makes a dash and John turns and holds up a hand, but it's Geraldine who catches Cara by the arm, before she comes into physical contact with her husband.

Sam shouts up at the camera. Just the top of Ollie's head is visible, his brother protecting his body with his own.

'It's locked! It's locked! I haven't got a key!'

'I can't hear you, Sam,' his father calls into the intercom grille, looking intensely at Geraldine.

'I said it's locked! Please!' The young voice comes through distorted and metallic.

'I still can't hear you.'

'The shutters!'

'I can't hear you saying sorry, Samuel.'

'... What? Dad! Please, it's getting worse and worse, there's stuff flying everywhere, we can't even see.'

Ollie turns and shouts in his brother's ear. Sam shakes his head. Then Ollie wriggles out from his brother's arms and tilts his face up to the camera.

'We went to their house and we couldn't even find it!' He snorts up tears and snot and rain. 'Why couldn't they come in with us?'

Cara can't believe John's face, then, which looks surprised, and amused. Quite calmly, quite without urgency, he calls into the intercom, 'Oh, Oliver. I explained – I'll tell you the whole conversation we had, you'll see, he agreed with me in the end, it was for the best –'

'You're lying, like you always lie!'

Cara can see Sam saying his brother's name over and over, tugging his shoulder.

'Now, young man, I don't think you're in any position –'

'You don't care about anyone and you never did. It's all your fault. Everything at home. You ruined everything so that no one can live there properly, just to make money!'

Sam manages to pull Ollie away from the intercom. 'Look, Dad, we're sorry, okay? Please, open the shutters?'

John's shoulders relax. 'You must understand, boys, rules exist for good reason. You can't run wild.'

'Tell them it's because we love them so much, John.'

'Your mother has been absolutely beside herself.'

Geraldine drops Cara's arm and goes to the sofa. Cara steps forward. Now she can see properly: the plastered hair, the teeth chattering in the hot September night. The wide-eyed expectation of the two young boys, who have still not been let in.

'OK. We're sorry.'

'Oliver? Put Oliver on.'

'... Sorry.'

You can hear they mean it.

'Very good,' says their father. 'But there'll be no football for two weeks. And no PlayBox.'

'Fine! OK!'

'No taking the rifle into the woods,' calls Geraldine from the sofa, and John repeats this for the boys' benefit. They accept every sanction. Then, finally, with the wind now drowning out even their shouts, John presses the button and lets the children in.

Michaela moves off into the Atlantic before dawn. The drop

in the wind wakes Cara from her half-sleep, and she dozes in a sort of bliss. Knowing there is devastation somewhere, but that it's not where she is, gives her a very base type of joy: the lions have taken the slowest, but she escaped with the herd.

Monday morning is still the stormiest Cara has ever known – when she opens the shower window to see what's happening, her face receives a warm slap of wet and she quickly shuts it again – but it's not in the same league as last night. There's thunder, but the animal storm now sounds caged. The generator's back on – it had just tripped its over-heat switch – and when she finds clean water still running from the taps, the $30 bottle of imported handsoap smug on the uncracked basin, she knows everything'll be all right for them.

She's forgotten to put the maple syrup on the table and she's glad of an excuse to pop to the kitchen. For once, all five of them are eating together; the boys slept too late for breakfast, so this is brunch. While the rain batters down there isn't much else they can do. She's made a homely tableful: pancakes, sweet and savoury; a pile of crispy bacon; toast in a basket covered with a linen cloth; and a bowl of leftover fruit salad jazzed up with some Sprite. Even Geraldine takes a pancake from the warm stack, but some-how they seem hungry as individuals rather than a group.

She comes back with the syrup and Sam perks up, reach-ing for the bottle. Ollie says no and pushes his plate away half-finished. She excuses herself to start the washing-up.

Geraldine comes in with her empty mug and plate. 'Should be easing off before long,' she shouts.

'Yep,' says Cara, scrubbing hard at the crusted griddle.

The day sags, drags. The garden is strewn with debris, and one of the upper shutters has come loose, letting in a swaying triangle of grey light. Now the worst has passed she's just waiting for the world to restart. In the meantime, there's this kind of anticlimactic trough, like sitting in an empty bath. While Geraldine and John are watching a film, she goes and knocks on Sam's door.

He's propped up on the bed playing Permakult. The PlayBox ban lasted only as long as John and Geraldine could stand the boys slumping silently in the living room. Cara picks up the second controller and together they destroy a logging facility in the Amazon. She wonders why Ollie's not there, whether they've fallen out, but Sam says his brother just had 'other stuff to do'.

She knocks, as always. Ollie's standing by his bed when she opens the door.

'What are you up to, lovey?'

'Nothing.'

'Don't you want to play a bit of Permakult with us?'

'It's all right.'

His body is indicating something under the bed. She's sorry he wants to hide it, after he'd been open enough to show her that incredible collage before, but maybe he's angry with her, too.

She sits on the end of the bed and pats the Transformers duvet, and he sits, shoulders forward. His hair sticks up all tufty from the night.

'You know, I'm sure your Mum and Dad didn't realise how bad it was out there.'

He doesn't move.

'They were so worried – I was so worried! – when you didn't come back.'

Still nothing.

'What happened, Oll? Lovey? Did you forget about the storm?'

'No! Course not. We went to look for him. You know. Then it was just – the storm started and we got stuck, and it took ages to get home. Nothing happened.'

'Well, I know you were worried about Jean-Chrétien, but everyone was panicking. I think your Mum and Dad just wanted to make sure you knew you mustn't do anything like that again.'

These words are growing in size as they come out of her mouth, like in a dream of spitting out endless broken teeth.

'I know.' It's not just the sigh of a sorry child. There's someone new in there, too, someone she doesn't yet know.

'I'm sure they were fine. We'd have heard.'

He looks at her. She looks away.

'Ollie, there are things grown-ups do that you don't understand when you're young.' Even as she says it, she feels sick, and she doesn't blame him for not answering.

When she leaves him, she slips into the utility room and checks the gun is there, locked in its case.

A week later Cara and the boys have repaired the guttering, cleared a large section of the garden, and heaved the emptied-out water barrels back into place by the shed. Realising again the power that tipped them over when they were full makes her shudder. Fourteen people were killed on the out-islands, but it sounds as if, so far, their island has got away with no fatalities.

The sun's out again as if nothing has happened.

Jean-Chrétien came back to work today, too. When he arrived she dashed out, greeted him with a breathless 'Hi!' and 'How is everything?' which makes her cringe now. She'd imagined that one day they'd share an understanding, that he'd see they were in the same boat: two refugees slaving for the ones who have a choice – though as soon as she formulated this thought, she was overcome with shame. He nodded and said, 'Hello, Ma'am,' but his face was so different without its smile. He has been quiet even around the boys. Ollie stood near him, waiting to be invited alongside, but the gardener didn't stop raking detritus from the lawn.

Working outside for the last few days seems to have calmed the boys – Sam is almost cheerful. Maybe they're a bit monosyllabic with their parents, but things will smooth over soon.

She's putting away Ollie's ironing when she notices the encyclopedia sticking out from under the bed. She knows she shouldn't, but she wants to see, to enjoy his talent for herself. As she pulls out the heavy book it knocks against something else. His laptop.

It's open and awake on her knee. It just happened. Now she's reading an illustrated blog post, dated yesterday, by 'Ol-Ell'. The blog's logo is a green-balaclava-clad head and shoulders, a rifle up at an angle by the face. She skim-reads between the infamous photos of the Bowland protest aftermath, and images from the first bad day of vapour, when boats were evacuated all along the Thames. There are other photos, of babies that shouldn't really have been allowed to live, some graphs of WarmUtil profits, diagrams of shale layers and the paths of leached fluids, and a lot of capital letters in the prose.

The poisoning took years, developing accusations and denials and counter-denials and finally real evidence, by which time it was too late. Patients inundated their GPs with complaints of exhaustion, hair loss, persistent abscesses. They left undiagnosed. Thousands of couples failed to conceive but didn't come forward for years, assuming they were exceptional. Cancer clusters started to spike regional health graphs like geysers, and still no one could definitively prove why.

Fingers began to point at companies like WarmUtil and their subsidiaries. And the governments who'd granted the extraction contracts in the first place. They had, all of them, acted in defiance of the petitions, the marches, the gate-shackle protests (in Bowland, most memorably) and it was clear who the bad guys were when you didn't think about it closely. But looking at the cash the Ellands give her for groceries, and what she's managed to put away as savings, Cara does think about it closely. Even though he's too young to remember Bowland, Ollie clearly thinks about it too.

After five minutes of her heart trying to escape her throat, she snaps Ollie's laptop closed and goes to the window. He's down there, kicking the displaced gravel back onto the path one piece at a time. It's inefficient and charming and he looks eleven years old.

For eighteen months she's stewed the same thoughts, accepting her part in the collective blame, but wondering when it was, exactly, that everyone agreed to this irreparable violence. Only now is she beginning to crystallise the thing Ollie can see straight and true: the betrayal of his generation. If she were him, she would be murderous.

The main road has been clear since a few days after the hurricane, but the off roads that go into the bush and toward the water are still strewn with shredded plant matter. In places, whole stands of shallow-rooted trees have tipped into the roadway as one, as if they'd made a mutual agreement to resist the storm for only so long. Cara had to force the Jeep through the sandy verge to get by, and the altered landscape caused her to miss the little open area where she usually parks with the boys; once she realised, she had to reverse slowly until she found it.

There are certain things Cara needs to settle for herself before she takes irreversible action. There are some packed bags in the spare bedroom wardrobes. There is enough time left on her US visa. Her plan has taken a lot of preparation, and this, today, is a last part of it.

She opens the passenger door, takes the rifle from its case and picks her way over the tangled brush. Even with the sighing casuarinas, it's so quiet that the visual chaos seems falsely still, like a frieze she's found herself able to walk around in. But she finds the spot, the boys' log still just where it was despite the hurricane. Just out of sight, the sea continues its forever business, the water here clean to the naked eye.

She may, embarrassingly, not know how to empty the pellets from the barrel or chamber or whatever it's called, but she's seen enough to know how to fire. She lies on her stomach like a sniper and holds the weapon the way she's seen the boys do it. It feels huge. Then, as she adjusts to its weight, *she* feels huge. She pumps it and aims at the log. It's thrilling. She moves a shaking finger to the trigger. But wait. She might as well do this with style. It doesn't take her long to find a bottle in the undergrowth. She balances it on the log and goes back to her position.

She squeezes the trigger and fires. There's a flash of John's face which she blinks away. The bottle stands, glinting green, but sand puffs up encouragingly close. She might be good at this.

The other afternoon, after no sleep the night before, she waited until John – back in his barely interrupted routine – was snoozing, and went to Geraldine. She was in the living room, plumping cushions Cara had already plumped.

'Do you think Ollie's... okay?' Cara said from the doorway.

'Oh, Oliver's going through a *phase*.'

'Do you think? Only, he's been so quiet, you know, after the other night.'

'He's hitting puberty, poor boy. I shouldn't worry, they're both thinking about their genitals most of the time.'

'I don't know. There was this thing I saw...' She'd stopped, not wanting to betray him.

'I know all about it!' Geraldine picked up a magazine and tucked herself down into an armchair.

'You know?'

'Of course. Dear me, Cara, they are my own boys. "A mother knows",' she said, leafing. 'He draws these ghastly pictures, some sort of dystopian awfulness with lots of black – you know how boys that age get all romantic about war and fantasy worlds and so on. He showed me one the other day, and I told him being idealistic is all very well, but when he starts living in the real world he'll see.'

'Oh.'

She looked up. 'Oh dear. Was I awful? I probably should

have been more encouraging. I forget how young he is. Though at his age I was doing four languages.'

Cara aims at the bottle. She has no idea how many pellets are in this thing. She fires. Even though she misses again, it feels as if something has been struck, hard. The sheer speed with which it all happens, and the noise. Like she can crack open the world.

She talked to Geraldine again, light-voiced, saying she was worried the boys still weren't really talking to their father, that everyone probably needed a break, and Geraldine leapt at the chance to come over to Fort Lauderdale. They're going early tomorrow. After Customs they'll part: Cara's flying off with the boys to Boston, then driving them north, all the way up into Maine, to the national park at Acadia. It's one of the last wilds, one of the last places you can find somewhere quiet to stay without registering on the grid. Though it would be good to have something for protection, she knows she can't take the rifle – with no firearms licence, she might just about get it onto a plane here but there's no way she'd get it into the States. It's for the best.

If Geraldine comments on the amount of luggage, well, a trip like that needs serious stuff: the very best camping gear; clothes for wet weather, hot weather, cold; beast-proofing equipment. Their mother isn't likely to dig deeper, not until she realises they're not back when they said they'd be. They'll be carrying all the intangible stuff she's prepared, too: mp3 playlists for the hire car, photos of their parents on a memory stick – she's not cruel, she knows there is a lot of love there as well – and her knowledge, the absolute knowledge, that this is the right thing for them. Everything else, like schooling, new names if need be, she'll worry about when the time comes.

She shifts to make herself a better hollow in the sand. She fires again. Then again and again, and again. It's fun. It is. It could run away with you, this passion. The boys know it in their young limbs – it's spreading fast through them, and it's spreading through her, right now, hot streaks of adrenalin that she wants to pursue. But. She's the grown-up. She has to keep on top of it for all their sakes, has to set herself against destruction, even though destruction has become the overwhelming force. Just as she has to take them away, even though there isn't any real away to take them to.

It's not a perfect plan, of course – the boys might come to hate her, especially Ollie. It's not even logical: she's acting as if she can protect them like they're her own children, when they're not, and she can't. All she can be sure of is that they deserve better. Her, too.

She fires and the pellet just pings the bottle, and though it doesn't shatter, it's knocked down, thuds into the sand. She gets up and resites it, goes back to her prone position. She finds another level of stillness she didn't know she had. Looking along the barrel, breath held, making the longest, slowest, calmest possible squeeze of the trigger, she fires again and this time it's dead on and the bottle shatters, as if from its own power, dust and shards of green glass arcing in the air.

She lets her breath out in a huff of pleasure, finds an echo of the hunger still there for one more shot. She tries again, aiming at nothing, but when she tugs at the trigger this time there's just a click.

Climbing to her feet, she drops the neutered weapon to

the ground, then takes the car jack from the boot of the Jeep and starts to hit and hit. Even with her weak and trembling shooting arms the rifle's soon in bits. Driving back, she stops at three separate bins and drops the pieces in.

[SUPERFAR]

Dear Robyn,

Thanks for your letter. Still cant believe this works! (Can you send some more of your 'paper'? This is the last slice.)

Reading about your 'trip' was way buzzy. Tell me more stuff!! Its like since your letter I got this brainthirst. I did a sneaky Old-Era interro but couldnt find much, + anyway, you say it better, youre actually back there.

What news from here... well... Net Pop is up by 12, which is good, I think were getting over the parasite thing. They changed the airfilters – I mean it was scheduled + everything, but it meant 2000 pips of Low-Oxy Podtime, which, ugh. Otherwise... boring.

Explain how you do your seenery. Is it like totally, 110% convincing? How is it powered? I loved that bit you said about the mountainal area you went to and it had loads of like outside water you could actually touch forreal? Mazing.

But though, so, how do you deal with being

atmospherically compromised for any long clocktime? Bet youre paying for it now, right?! I was outside for like 10 pips once, when we had a total de-contam after this really nasty burster? + I just vommed straight off + got this sledding head-ache for like a week or whatever.

Must be so weird living like you guys.

I cant stop thinking about what you put, that long bit about how you got really high up, and your eyes were some-how seeing superfar, with all the greenings laid out before you like a mazing deepscreen, but forreal? And how there was like a freshness + a rightness in it and in you, like you + it were part of the same thing? Its funny, I sortof knew what you meant. It was nice, and but also, it kindof hurt a little bit?

Write back,

Ro81N

Dear Robyn,

I know! But Im so full of queries for you too. I will try to
describe my activities in + out of Pod, but how to do it when
your lifes so much more entrancing?! Like woah, youre not
talking about a forreal horse? That you got on top of it +
let it move you around? Talk about Unknown. But must be
mazing I guess.

I will answer your Qs but, worryface, answers are boring
with no horses so maybeso you wont want to bother sending
anymore slices to your boring 'friend'.

I say 'friend' cos this is like were chatting but youre not on
my ladder at all, not even i*i? (I mean even the podswabbers
are i*i with us, ha ha.) Which is weird, like Im dreaming you.
So pls send your icon asap if you can get it thru. Heres mine,
I just made it simple 3helix format so hopefully you can pick
it up and we can be i*i for a start. Then we can Formalize.
Though, thinking, thats maybeso not such a great idea since
this is kindof definitely forreal what theyd call an Informal
Channel! And shutdown.

Alrightyso, to answer your Qs.

1: yes.

2: yes.

3: sort of, but probably not like you guys.

4: no!

5: about 98 pips out of 100, then the other 2 out of Pod,
though thatd be silly so its more like say 500 pips in, 20 out
kindof thing then back in for 1000 or whatever.

6: yeah, I dont totally know how. But not a 'pen' like you
said about. Right now Im strapt in Pod, writing to you, just
like I do everything strapt in Pod (except activities out of Pod

obvs), but so okay to write to you its pretty simple, I have seers On and transmit On, and stem function on High, and then I just get the paper slice laid over my flatscreen and its hello world! If I want to change something I just zed it off, maybe you could try that as I see in your letters there is scrubbling mess everywhere.

7: Your Big Q. Okay so I know this roughly (its just Basic Awareness) but Id have to apply for an interro to get more. But the thing is, I get this twistiness when I think about you not knowing now, like youre a baby all sweet, + then me telling you + you not being a baby anymore.

Some pips later... You wont believe this Robyn but I had to stop writing then for wetface + judders. It took awhile to become dry + still. That hasnt happened since I was in a miniPod! I shoct myself but somehow I can tell you, I guess I know you wont Report to the emmos.

I def dont want to see that Urgency emmo again – lastime it probed me right through the flatscreen and it was not gentle! Sharp scratch it says, then before you can brace down its pulled out your seers + hearers + youre being acidflusht like a mofo. Right? I guess weve all been thru it. Specially those parasited 1s. Though it turned out that, for them, even triple-flushing didnt stop them getting to Burst point. Sadface.

As you can tell my words are getting v small now, no space, so will say AddYou. Write back. Ro81N

Dear Robyn,

Well it was super to see that flat of what you look like facially. Now Im a little glad you couldnt see mine. Why were you worried? If any1 back there says you dont meet standards then they must have infected seers! Or stem function at like zero. Ive never seen any1 so complete.

Im just sorry I cant screen it up, + I mean Ive tried every which thing. So for now youre still not on my ladder. This is not a problem for me, understand! To me you are not Unknown. Its just that as I said lastime were dangling heavily over the edge of this being an Informal Channel. I guess were so Informal its not even lighting anything up! Im surprised your ends still working too, with what you said about Mydad 'tidying up' your wires + loops + every1 using the Micro Wave all the time.

What I shouldof said first off was, you look very nice (see, Ive been studying the way you guys Related). But I can tell anyway that youre very nice, because youre living with Other people all around you right so close you can touch, which, wow, mazing. There must be so much fleshtrust there all between you, where you know 110% that youre clean + theyre clean. You do know, right, forreal? Dont make me worry.

Now get ready, this is a crazy Q, but do you even sleep unloct?? That would seriously undermine my snoozing pips! Being unloct, with the chance an Other might get in + end me? No way. Me, Im triple-bolted + password-encrypted. Sometimes, if we have no out of Pod pips upcoming, I dont even unbolt, Im just happy strapt in Pod, loct down + humming.

Anyway. Look at you, you dont need me telling you how

to stay safe in your quaint Old Era 'enviro'.

I might be sorry after this bit, but I somehow feel like pips are getting low + you did say about your end maybe stopping due to Mydad. So though I havent done an interro I will try to answer your big Q now.

Will probably use 2 slices.

Thinking, its sortof like the Tale of You + Me, because its the Tale of you ending + me beginning (though actually I think there was a humungous long row of pips in between, with a load of dark fire + stuff before we workt out what to do?) but its still kindof like a string between us. So here it goes. So.

So anyway in Basic Awareness they say about a kindof ideal operating system which had everything all alive + fitting smoothly together in all dimensions, which actually from your 1st letter with the seenery + stuff I can kindof understand a bit. Which then we, or you, or some1 or 1s (unclear) did something (unclear) over a period of pips (unclear! – they totally blur over a superload of detail! But theyd have to, right? I mean no-1 wants all that super-com-putercom graph shit, specially if it looks bad, I mean total bummer headache). + anyway, for those load of pips it seemed like nothing was wrong + it must be the supercom just being a massive buzzkill or whatever. Then you, or they or whoever, lookt around + saw a load of things were wrong + couldnt be right again + all the stuff you (or they/whoever) needed to be all alive + nice were gone or about to be gone.

Then it was all oh shit better do something, then all well we cant its too late, then no seriously we better do something, but then in the end the bad sortof like tipt. + then it was just a massive party opportunity for the tiny invisible 1s, like hey come on little guys, theyre too busy fighting, we are so good at dancing our nasty dance in peoples eyes + testines + heads, lets celebrate.

They came really fast so no-1 totally knows what bit happened when. But at some point you (they/whoevs) did massive massive exploding of massive stuff everywhere to try + make things better (??I know, right? but thats what it says) + then thats kindof the end of what I remember from Basic Awareness, but its basically the Tale of supergood, going superbad.

Sorry.

Though I say 'bad', I mean Im not whining, Im strapt in Pod nice + clean, no Infections recently in my area, I passt all my emmo inspections (so far!!!) + theres so much still to explore in my deepscreen. I have to say though that your world just seems. Different.

Write back.

Ro81N

ACKNOWLEDGEMENTS

Massive thanks to everyone at Boiler House Press, especially my editor Philip Langeskov whose incredible insights and skilful coaxing have much improved these stories. Thanks to my agent Euan Thorneycroft, for his unwavering optimism. For invaluable teaching, influence, and permission-giving, I owe thanks to Jacob Ross, Jon McGregor, Helen Oyeyemi and the late Becky Swift.

Gratitude to all my writer friends, and to helpful readers of early versions, especially Lindsay Waller-Wilkinson. Thanks to all competition readers, judges and magazine editors – to every champion of short fiction. Thank you to everyone at Spread The Word in London, past and present.

The personal and practical support of my non-writer friends has gone above and beyond. I count myself lucky every day to have you.

For their belief and love, thanks to my family.

Finally, thank you to C – who makes everything possible, with constancy and superhero-level kindness.

Earlier versions of some of these stories have appeared elsewhere: 'Edith Aleksander, b.1929' in *Aesthetica Creative Writing Annual 2015*; 'The Two-Body Problem' in *I Am Because You Are* (Freight Books); 'We Are Part of This' in *The Forge Literary Magazine*; 'Mating Week' in *The Bridport Prize 2012*, and in *I You He She It* (University of Huddersfield Press); 'The Ground is Considerably Distorted' in *Lighthouse*; 'Eliminate Toxins and Increase Blood Flow' in *The Pygmy Giant*, 'Biophile' in *The White Review*; 'Flamingo Land' in *Flamingo Land & Other Stories* (Flight Press); 'On Day 21' in *Wasafiri* online; '[Superfar]' in *The Letters Page* and in *The Lonely Crowd*.

The Formula in 'Flamingo Land' was provided by Colly Myers.